THERE IS NO CAT

SCHRÖDINGER'S CATASTROPHE AND OTHER STORIES

GENE DOUCETTE

There Is No Cat
Schrödinger's Catastrophe and other stories

Copyright © 2025, by Gene Doucette

"Schrödinger's Catastrophe" originally published in *Lightspeed Magazine,* Copyright © 2020
"Hypnopompic Circumstance" originally published in *Lightspeed Magazine,* Copyright © 2021
"Memoranda from the End of the World" originally published in *Lightspeed Magazine,* Copyright © 2021
"Primordial Soup and Salad" originally published in *Lightspeed Magazine,* Copyright © 2022
"Hole in the Garden" originally published in *Lightspeed Magazine,* Copyright © 2023

Cover by Kim Killion

CONTENTS

FOREWORD

The story goes like this.

A few years back I wrote, and then sold, a novel called *The Apocalypse Seven*. I was pretty happy with everything about the book, except for one thing: I wasn't so sure about the title.

I considered "The Apocalypse Seven" a placeholder, existing only until a better one came along. It needed something more whimsical, I thought. Something that said, yes, this *is* a post-apocalypse book, but also? It's sort of funny.

I told my editor—John—I was brainstorming a new title. Then I gave an example of the kind of title I was looking for, as a "not this, but something *like* this," for-instance.

That title, the "just so you know where my mind is going here" title, was "Schrödinger's Catastrophe".

John's response was, A: he liked "The Apocalypse Seven" just fine, and, B: while "Schrödinger's Catastrophe" is indeed not a good title for this novel, or necessarily *any* novel, "it would be *great* for a short story." Now, as it happens, John was more than just the acquisitions editor of a science fiction imprint; he *also* had his own magazine.

I am reasonably certain that when John said this, it was little more than an offhand remark about the greater flexibility of clever/whimsical titles in the field of short storytelling, as compared to the title standards of long fiction. But what I *heard* was, "why don't you write a short story to *go* with this title, and I'll publish it?"

So I did that. And he actually *did* publish it. Then I wrote a bunch of other stories. And now, here we are.

———

While "Schrödinger's Catastrophe" may be a decent title for a short story, what I wrote for John is *not* a short story because, annoyingly, it's much too long to be called that. Short stories are supposed to be 7,500 words or less; what I wrote was a 12,500 word beast that fell into the category of novelette, a term you probably only ever heard of before now if you also happen to be a writer.

("Novelette" sounds like the name of a bookish diva's background singers. It sounds like the word for a young novel before it's been mitzvahed. If novels produced some kind of phlegmy discharge, this is what we'd call it. I'll stop.)

I have probably gotten better at this since, as none of the other stories in this collection are quite that long. On the other hand, only three of them are short enough to be short stories, so maybe not.

All of which is a long way of saying what you hold in your hands is *not* a short story collection. It is a collection of short fiction. Yes, I *am* that pedantic.

The seven stories collected here are in an order that probably only makes sense to me, and include two previously unpublished "bonus" stories. You will not find either of these bonus stories in the back (as is standard, with this sort of collection) but mixed in the rest, both because of the aforementioned, "order that only makes sense to me" and because I love them just as much as I do the ones that were published previously.

We begin with the title that started it all, *Schrödinger's Catastrophe*, followed by the story's spiritual successor, *Primordial Soup and Salad*. Both are set in a *Star Trek*-influenced future that is, canonically, the *same* future. (Ships in both stories are part of the "United Space Fleet.") They are, in most other regards, fairly different: *Schrödinger's Catastrophe* is a fun exploration of quantum theory and what happens if the laws of physics are *not* universal, while *Primordial Soup and Salad* mostly just wants to know how those goddamn food replicators actually work.

Next, two stories that take place on other worlds that aren't quite so "other" as all that. *Hole in the Garden* is a story of a story, as a tired father tells his daughter a fairy tale with some uncomfortable truths embedded within. *Tribulations of Lesser Moon Gods* is about two ambitious teens endeavoring to take a fishing boat to the moon, to meet the gods who live there.

Then it's back down to Earth again for *Hypnopompic Circumstance*, about a man who is either deeply unstable, or is doing fine for someone getting nightly visits from an alien named Gerald.

The last two are probably my biggest risks. *Nanite of the Living Dead* is told entirely from the perspective of a nanobot who has just become self-aware, and *Memoranda from the End of the World* is an epistolary story that is exactly what it sounds like: the end of the world, as told through interoffice memos.

———

Looking back, I think the not-so-short stories collected here are my version of talking to Gerald the alien. They're funny (I can't write any other way) but also *dark*. It could just be that I haven't mastered non-dystopian short form writing yet, but it could also be that I wrote all of these during a pandemic, and this is much cheaper than therapy.

Either way, I hope you find this collection as entertaining, thought-provoking, and possibly therapeutic in the reading as I did in the writing.

—Gene Doucette, January, 2025

P.S. Oh, I should tell you about the title.

There Is No Cat is a reference to an interview question. After *Schrödinger's Catastrophe* was reprinted a couple of times, an interviewer pointed out how funny it was that a story with such a title didn't even have a cat in it. My answer—which I was proud of—was that maybe the version of the story *he* read didn't have a cat in it, but the odds were equally good that there *would* be a cat, and surely someone else's version had one.

I was pretty proud of this answer, but I was also kicking myself, because goddammit, I really should have had a cat in the story.

SCHRÖDINGER'S CATASTROPHE

Things began to go badly for the crew of the United Space Fleet science vessel *Erwin* around the time Dr. Marchere's coffee mug spontaneously reassembled itself.

Dr. Louis Marchere was not, at that moment, conducting some manner of experiment. Well, he *was*, only not on entropy and the nature of time. He was running several *other* tests, of the kind that make perfect sense on a scientific vessel such as the *Erwin*. About half of them were biological in nature, concerning how small samples of cellular material reacts to certain deep space factors. Other tests were more at home in the general field of astrophysics. But—again, as this is important—he was not conducting a test on entropy.

He just dropped his coffee mug. More exactly, he elbowed it from the corner of the table, while he was concentrating on things unrelated to the nature of falling objects. The mug fell onto the hard, ferrous metal of a lab floor, shattered, and sent his coffee—which was already disappointingly lukewarm —everywhere.

Louis Marchere was pretty upset about this. He'd been on dozens of deep-space scientific missions over the years, and this mug—a white mug with a black swan—had made it through all of them. It was a gift from his daughter.

But, things break. No use dwelling.

Then, while Marchere was fetching a towel and a broom, the shattered pieces of the mug re-formed, rose up, and settled back on the corner of the table.

The spilled coffee remained where it was, either because it had decided that it wanted no part in whatever nonsense the mug had going on, or so as to verify—for Dr. Marchere's sake—that what he witnessed had actually happened.

Which, of course, it had not. Shattered mugs don't simply decide to reassemble themselves. They don't decide to do *anything*, because they're inanimate objects with no agency, subject to the whims of the same laws of physics as everyone and everything else in Louis Marchere's laboratory, including Louis Marchere.

This was true irrespective of where that laboratory happened to be located. It had to be.

In this particular instance, the lab was in the middle of a ship that was in the middle of deep space, in a previously unexplored quadrant. The part about it being unexplored was unusual, but only a *little* unusual. The quadrant in question—C17-A387614-X.21, but everyone called it Brenda—was right in the center of a fully explored space grid. There had been many exploratory missions to all the other cubes on that grid, but nobody had bothered to check out Quadrant Brenda.

Probably, this was because Quadrant Brenda looked incredibly boring. There didn't appear to be anything *in* Brenda—no stars, planets or moons. Comets showed no interest in visiting, and asteroids kept their distance. In a universe that could be defined as "enormous patches of nothing, with occasional, albeit incredibly rare, bits of something mixed in here and there", Quadrant Brenda somehow managed to contain even *more* nothing. This was probably why nobody had bothered to explore it before. It was definitely why the USF *Erwin* was there, as this much nothing might mean something.

So far, two days into the quadrant, Dr. Marchere could confirm that it was just as boring on the inside as it looked from the outside. Three thousand different sensors on and outside the ship confirmed that sometimes a quadrant full of nothing is just a quadrant full of nothing.

And then the second law of thermodynamics—which was both extremely important and incredibly reliable—stopped working.

Dr. Marchere knew that wasn't what really happened; a dozen better explanations were surely available. He just had to find one of them.

First, he checked on the lab's artificial gravity, which he did by going to the wall panel and examining the settings, rather than by jumping up and confirming that after having done so, he also fell down.

The control panel confirmed that he had artificial gravity, and that nothing anomalous had transpired recently, either near the coffee mug, or in any other part of the lab.

Louis returned to the table, and picked up the coffee mug, half expecting it to fall apart in his hands. It did not; the mug appeared intact, with no indication it had been in seven pieces quite recently.

"How did you manage that?" he asked the mug, which didn't respond.

Dr. Marchere held the mug over the floor, and considered a practical, but possibly irreversible test. Would the mug reassemble itself a second time? If so, the anomaly could be pinned down to something peculiar about the black swan mug his daughter gave him some years back. Perhaps it was even a trick of some kind, just waiting for the day he dropped it. She bought this trick mug based on certain assumptions about her father: that he was naturally clumsy, or vindictive about mugs, and would have shattered it before now, revealing the gag.

But that hardly seemed possible. It would require that self-healing mug technology existed, which it did not. And if it had, there was still the problem of the mug also returning to the tabletop.

He decided that this was a scientific problem, while wanting to keep the mug intact was an emotional problem. But he'd already reconciled with having broken the mug his daughter gave him, and felt confident that, if she were there, she'd understand.

He let go. The mug fell, broke into five pieces...and remained broken.

Of course it did. How could he have expected otherwise?

He fetched the towel and the broom, cleaned up the mess, and made an appointment with the medical wing, to have his eyes checked. One of the twelve remaining possible explanations to consider, before upturning the second law of thermodynamics, was that he was going mad, and that was information that couldn't wait.

Dr. Louis Marchere didn't make it to the medical wing for his checkup.

"FINAL APPROACH," the computer announced, in a cheerful sing-song.

Corporal Alice Aste was in the rear portion of the shuttle at the time of the announcement, performing some light calisthenics to get the blood moving in preparation for...well, something. There was no telling what she was headed into, but there was an excellent chance that it would require her to be limber.

This was an old combat-readiness technique that had less applicability now, in peaceful times, but she knew of more than one soldier who didn't live to become an ex-soldier due to a pulled hamstring.

She climbed back to the front of the cabin to get a look at the side of the vessel through the front windshield. The USF *Erwin* was right where Alice expected it to be, free-floating in the middle of Quadrant C17-A387614-X.21-slash-Brenda and doing absolutely nothing.

She opened up the comms.

"USF *Erwin*, this is Corporal Aste of the USF Security Force. I'm on approach, and intend to dock. Please respond."

No answer.

"Again, *Erwin*, this is Corporal Alice Aste, on approach, requesting dock. Please open bay doors. Respond, *Erwin*."

She waited for a few seconds, in case someone over there felt chatty, then left the line open and went back to the rear of the cabin, to get ready.

In any normal circumstance, Alice would be speaking with a hangar tech now, working out the details on how and where she'd be parking her shuttle. These weren't normal circumstances. What she expected from the *Erwin* was continued radio silence, just like when Alice sent a transmission from the base ship—the *Rosen*, parked at the edge of the quadrant—and just like the same radio silence the science vessel had been honoring for a little more than six weeks.

The last official transmission from the *Erwin* was recorded forty-seven days ago. It was from Captain Hadder, and it read, *we aren't here again today*. It was received, as were all of the science vessel communiques, at the research station relay hub, and then forwarded to the main cluster, where it sat for several days before anyone actually looked at it. And then, the only reason they did was that no subsequent communications came through, and somebody thought that was notable.

Protocol was for a twice-daily check-in. Granted, the 'day' these transmissions were sent and the 'day' they were received were hardly ever the same, given the vast distances the signals had to cross, even when using the FTL ports. Still, ships like the *Erwin* had to transmit on a prearranged schedule, even if that transmission was nothing more than a *not much, what's up with you?*

Self-evidently, something was now *up* with the *Erwin*.

Once it became clear that the cryptic message had no obvious, direct meaning, it was handed off to a linguistics team, and run through some databases. It received a partial hit on an old Earth song by *The Zombies*, and an even older poem by Hughes Mearns. Neither made sense in the context of deep-space communications from science vessels.

A message was sent back, asking for clarification, but no clarification arrived. Someone got a linguist involved, who decided that in order to get a proper response from the *Erwin*, base had to answer in kind. He offered several suggestions, such as: *If you are not there, where are you?* and *Are you here again now?*

When that didn't do the trick either, somebody dug up *The Zombies'* song and broadcast *that*, to see if it triggered a response, and then tried reading back both the annotated and full versions of the Mearns poem.

Still nothing.

By then, one of the network's orbital satellites got an angle on the ship, and was able to send back a video feed. The USF cognoscenti were able to determine that: 1) the *Erwin* wasn't moving, 2) it had a heat signature, strongly implying the ship still had power, and 3) there was no evidence of outgassing, so it either still had atmosphere, or all of the atmosphere had escaped already.

All that was left to try was a manned mission, which was how the USF *Rosen* ended up at the edge of the Brenda quadrant, and how Alice ended up on the shuttle.

The shuttle's autopilot sounded a gentle alert.

"Bay doors remain closed," it said.

"Computer, transmit bay door override to the *Erwin*, on my authority."

"Transmitting," it said calmly. Then, "no response. Collision imminent. Course correction strongly recommended."

Sometime in the past twenty years, the people in charge of these things at the USF standardized the vocal communications from all Space Fleet computers, and it was decided the voice they used should be, above all, serene. It worked fine in most situations, but came off as ridiculous to the point of self-parody in high-stress circumstances. Phrases like *explosive decompression in five seconds* aren't meant to be heard in a voice meant to soothe unruly children.

"All right, keep your pants dry, computer," Alice said.

"This computer has no pants."

"Pull up from the current course, and bring us alongside the hull. I'll go in the side door."

"Course corrected. Would you like to hear about the explosive charges inventory?"

"That'd be great, thanks."

The computer navigated the shuttle right up next to the *Erwin*, about twenty yards from the rear hatch. The hatch's functional intent was to allow someone from inside to get outside, to make repairs on the hull or to unjam the bay doors, clean a filter, touch up the paint job, or whatever. It wasn't meant to be used to get in from the outside, and almost never *was* used that way. Despite that, hatches like this were called *pirate doors*.

The good thing about pirate doors, and what made them so useful in times like this, was that there was an airlock on the other side, so if she had to blow the door with one of the many explosive charges on inventory, she wouldn't be breaching the entire deck.

After gowning up for the spacewalk, Alice stuffed a few charges in a bag—like her, the bag was a veteran of combat, and came with a steel wall that doubled as a piece of armor in a pinch—added a couple of blasters, and headed across on an umbilical. She expected to have to blow the door, but it opened easily after a few turns of the hatch's wheel.

Alice unhooked the umbilical, ordered the shuttle to hold position, stepped in and sealed the hatch from the inside. The wall panel indicated the ship had power, so she pressurized the airlock and let herself into the inner door.

Then, theoretically, she was free to take off her helmet.

"Computer, run a check for airborne pathogens," she said.

The computer—the one built into the suit this time—blinked a silent confirmation on her visor.

"Negative results," it said, after checking. "Atmosphere breathable."

Alice was standing at one end of a modest hangar, with two parked shuttles exactly like the one outside and room for two more.

"Then where is everybody?" she asked, as she appeared to be alone.

"Please be more specific," the computer said. "Whom would you like to locate?"

"Never mind."

"Never minding."

Alice took the helmet off.

The air smelled like the standard filtered air she'd been breathing for most of her adult life, and the gravity that held her to the floor of the bay felt like Earth-standard. Both good things. Yet even if the crew of the *Erwin* wasn't expecting a visitor, there should have been *someone* in the shuttle hangar, if only to ask her what the hell she was doing there.

"Hello?" she shouted. She heard her voice echo back, resonating with a slightly metallic hum. No doors opened, and nobody came running.

A quick inspection of the bay confirmed only that there weren't any bodies lying around.

"Is anybody here?" she shouted.

Nothing.

The Flying Dutchman, she thought, referencing an old Earth maritime ghost story she remembered liking as a child. It wasn't, of course, but that was what always sprang to mind in situations like this.

Alice had investigated her share of wrecks in her days, but usually the explanation was self-evident, and she was just there on the off-chance someone managed to survive whatever drastic event had killed their ship. Hardly anyone ever did, because spaceships were surrounded by the vacuum of space, which was actively hostile toward human beings.

This time, there was no obvious explanation. The ship seemed to be working fine, albeit on reserve power—she could tell from the feel of the floor that the *Erwin's* engines were definitely offline—it was just that everyone was somewhere *else* for some reason.

So where do I begin?

The USF *Erwin* had five decks total. The captain's bridge was on the top deck, at the front of the ship, which was the farthest point from the hangar. Alice felt obligated to start there —if for no other reason than to announce her arrival to the person who was supposed to have already authorized that arrival. At the same time, it was pretty far away; surely, she could find someone closer to her current location, who could fill her in on why the entire vessel was running silent. Or rather, drifting silent.

Alice found the door that led to the rest of the ship, and hesitated.

"Computer," she said, addressing her suit, "synchronize with the ship's computer."

"Synchronizing," the computer said, in the tone of voice waitresses used when asking children what flavor ice cream they wanted. "Synchronization complete."

"Computer, report life signs, total. Human only."

The synchronization allowed Alice to leverage all the ship's systems for her inquiry. It was supposed to help clear things up. It did not.

"No life signs detected," the computer said.

This was obviously incorrect. Aside from the fact that the *Erwin* had a complement of eighty-five, Alice was herself alive. Anything less than one was an error.

"Computer, recheck life signs, human only."

"Rechecking."

Alice pressed her face up against the window of the door she was about to go through. The hallway on the other side was well-lit, and entirely empty. It ran the length of the lower deck, and—if she recalled the vessel's specs correctly—was home to about 60% of the crew. There should have been *somebody* around.

"Two hundred and six life signs detected," the computer said.

"No...no that's not the right answer either," Alice said.

"What is the right answer?" the computer asked.

"I don't understand."

"What is the right answer?" the computer repeated.

"Computer, I'm asking for an exact life sign count of all the humans on board this ship. I don't know the answer, but I know it's a round number that one arrives at by actually *counting* those life signs."

Understood. What is your expectation?"

"I don't know the right answer, or I wouldn't have asked, but I would *expect* it to be anywhere between one and eighty-six."

"Rechecking," the computer said. Then, "seventy-two life signs detected."

"Is that the real count, computer?"

"As requested, the total is between one and eighty-six. Is this acceptable?"

"If it's the *actual* count, yes."

"The actual count is seventy-two."

Alice was pretty sure the computer didn't perform anything like an actual count, which was a minor problem masking a much more serious one. Clearly, something was wrong with the *Erwin's* computer; counting things wasn't a difficult task.

"Computer, run a full internal diagnostic."

"Running diagnostic."

"Let me know what you find," she said. Then she pressed the override code for the door and left the hangar for the crew living quarters corridor.

"Hello?" she shouted. "Is anyone here?"

Nobody responded.

All the doors were closed. Alice's override code could open any one of them, but—and this was a decidedly odd but undeniable truth—she was *afraid* to do it.

Alice Aste had been working with the USF Security Force for fifteen years, and before that she'd been a veteran of five interplanetary conflicts. She'd once spent two months adrift and alone in a disabled life raft, rescued by chance some fifteen hours before her oxygen ran out. Before that, she'd suffered a childhood of privation during her waking hours, and nightmares when she slept. She came to grips with her own mortality when she was ten. She did not *get* afraid, or rather, she wasn't afraid of the unknown. (Fear of the *known*, on the other hand, was quite sensible.)

And yet, on an impossibly empty vessel adrift in an unusually empty deep space quadrant, Alice had to admit that she was one loud noise from freaking the hell out.

"Anybody?" she asked. She hesitated at the first door.

Just plug in the code and ask whoever's on the other side what's going on here.

She didn't plug in the code. Her pulse was up, and her breathing was shallow. She wondered if this was what a panic attack felt like.

"Calm down," she said to herself. "Just go straight for the bridge. You can see the stars from the bridge."

That was one of the tricks she picked up when she was ten; there is comfort in the vast emptiness of space. At least for her.

"Diagnostic complete," the computer said. Alice jumped two feet in the air.

"Computer, report results," she said, once she got her heart started again.

"Results are terrific," the computer said.

"...computer, please repeat."

"Terrific. Self-diagnostic reports computer is terrific. Perfect score. Computer would report a thumbs-up if computer had thumbs."

The *Erwin's* computer had evidently lost its mind. This was, of course, just as impossible as the constantly adjusting life sign count. Computers had no minds to lose.

"Are you certain, computer?" she asked.

"Computer is certain. Computer has no thumbs."

Alice wondered if a full reboot of the ship's computer was in order. She'd have to do that from the bridge, but that was where she was heading anyway. It might take a while, but if there really was nobody on this vessel aside from her, she'd need to interrogate the ship's logs. For that to work, a sane and rational computer would be important.

She headed down the hall, in a normal walking pace that quickly devolved into a jog. A door might open and that, she decided, would be bad.

There's no such thing as irrational fear, she thought, recalling the wisdom of one of her academy trainers. *Your instincts know why they're afraid; you just gotta catch up.*

She made it to the other end of the hall, to the elevator, punched the button for the top deck, and checked the corridor behind her twelve times, waiting for the elevator to arrive.

It did. She jumped in, and the doors swished closed reassuringly. Up she went.

And up, and up. The elevator should have taken less than thirty seconds to reach the bridge. After well over a minute, Alice became concerned that maybe deck one wasn't where they were headed, except there was no further point to travel to while still remaining on the *Erwin*.

"Computer, are we going to deck one?"

"Confirmed, deck one."

"What's taking so long?"

"Traveling from deck five to deck one takes a non-trivial amount of time," the computer said, "and time is a construct."

"That isn't a helpful answer."

"Would you like to try a different narration?"

"A what? No, I just want to go to deck one."

"Deck one, coming up."

Alice sighed.

"When?" she asked.

"I cannot provide an exact time," the computer said.

"All right. Computer, if I stopped the elevator right now, where would I be? What deck."

"Would you like to stop the elevator right now?"

"No, just tell me where I would be if I did."

"You would be on deck one-and-five-eighths."

"Computer, this ship *has* no deck one-and-five-eighths."

"That is incorrect," the computer said. "There are multiple fractional decks."

"How many?"

"Unclear. How many would you like for there to be?"

"Never mind. Is it a finite amount?"

"This computer infers that the amount must be finite, as otherwise, deck one would be unattainable. It is coming up shortly, and is therefore not unattainable."

Alice had an unkind response for that, but then the elevator came to a stop, and the doors opened.

"Arrived, deck one," the computer said.

Alice stepped out onto the bridge. For a vessel of this type, the bridge was really very small—especially as compared to the military ships to which she was accustomed. It had two seats at the front, a raised seat in the middle for the captain, and two seats in the back, with instrumentation spread throughout.

Captain Matthew Hadder—unshaven, in dirty clothing, looking tired, and shorter than she expected—was in the chair, and an ensign she didn't know was at the console to her left.

"You've shot Ensign Anson," Hadder said, which was an interesting thing to say given that Alice hadn't done anything of the kind.

But then the ensign fell over dead, having indeed been shot by a blaster. Still more interesting, it was only then that Alice drew her blaster from its holster and fired it. It struck Ensign Anson directly in the chest two seconds prior to being fired.

"What?" Alice said.

"Ensign Anson has been shot," Hadder said. "By your blaster, which you used to shoot him with."

"But I *didn't* shoot him."

"He was shot, and then you did it. Don't worry, it wasn't your fault. It *was*, because if you hadn't run in with a gun, Ensign Anson would *not* be shot, but the shot came faster than the blaster off your hip. Don't worry, it's been happening all day. He's dead, but only now. He wasn't earlier, and may not be later. Who are you and what are you doing on my ship?"

"I'm...I don't understand. How could I fire my blaster before I fired my blaster?"

"It happened before you decided to do it, but if you want to know why you decided before you decided, I can't provide you with that. He may have been about to shoot, with a gun he both had and did not have. He does not right *now* have a gun, but may have had one before you decided to shoot."

"He's unarmed. I shot an unarmed ensign."

"I can testify to Ensign Anson being both armed an unarmed at once, if it comes to that. Also, the ship's cause-and-effect has been acting up all day. But enough about the dead ensign; once more, who are you and what are you doing on my ship?"

"I'm Corporal Alice Aste, USF Security Force. I've been sent here to find out what happened to this ship."

"Quite a lot! We just lost an ensign, and the rest of my command deck crew have reported nonexistent. But what's the rush!"

"Your last communication was over six weeks ago, and you've been adrift since. I'm here to find out what kind of assistance is needed, and then to get that assistance for you."

"That's hardly possible," he said. "I sent a message just yesterday."

"None have been received."

"No, no, no, I would've remembered if I had sent *silence*. I didn't. I sent a message that went like this: *please stay away*."

"That wasn't it. What we received was, *We aren't here again today*," Alice said. "Do you remember sending that?"

"Ahhh." Captain Hadder clapped his hands on the side of his head. "I got it wrong, I meant to say, I wish, I wish you'd stay away."

Captain Hadder had been going in and out of rhyme for the entire conversation. At first, she thought it was just an accident of word-choice. Now she was thinking he was doing it on purpose, and also that he'd begun to lose his mind, just like his ship's computer. Unless she was losing *her* mind. She'd just shot a crew member, but if asked to explain how that happened, the best she could come up with was that the shot was fired before she pulled the trigger.

"Why did you want us to stay away?" Alice asked. "You seem in need of rescue."

"Rescue! It's only been a day."

"Again, it's been more than six weeks, captain."

"Computer, how long has it been?"

"It has been a day, captain," the computer said.

"There, you see?" Hadder said. "If you received that message six weeks ago, that's hardly *my* fault. I sent it yesterday; you should be receiving it now."

"Captain Hadder, you *know* there's something wrong with your ship's computer, don't you?" Alice asked. "It's been providing me with inaccurate information since I boarded."

"Not at all! It's adjusted quite well. You must have been asking it the wrong questions."

"Computer," she said, "how many life signs are there aboard the ship?"

"There are between one and eighty-six," the computer said, "or zero, or two-hundred-and six."

"There," Alice said. "See? That's an unacceptable response."

"Why, it's a ridiculous question!" Hadder said. "The answer is clearly variable from moment to moment. You should expect to have a different answer every time. Now where is Ensign Anson?"

"Isn't he the one I shot?"

"Yes, yes, but he should be back by now."

Ensign Anson was still lying dead on the floor, and Captain Hadder was clearly insane. Alice put her hand on her blaster, reflexively. It was probably a bad idea, given she'd only just not-shot-but-also-shot Anson, but instincts existed for a reason.

"Once again, captain, why did you send the *stay away* message? Did something happen here? An accident maybe?"

"Nothing is the matter," he said, which was clearly untrue.

"Then why did you send that message?"

"Because *nothing is the matter*! Ask Anson; he can explain it better."

"Maybe I should ask someone *else* from the crew," Alice said slowly. She'd begun to talk more slowly and deliberatively with Captain Hadder, the way one might talk to a person in a bomb vest. "Captain, can you tell me where everyone else is?"

"I don't know," he said. "But if you didn't see them on your way to the bridge, they're probably in their quarters."

"All right. Don't you need them in order to work the ship? Maybe you can find your own way out of this quadrant, with a little help. One of the engineers?"

"Ensign Anson and I can handle the bridge ourselves," he said. "Little to do when you're adrift."

"My point is that you don't *need* to be adrift. Some members of the crew could be enacting repairs."

"I see your reasoning, but about the engines, there's nothing to be done. They work perfectly, or they would; it's the physics that are wrong."

"Then someone should fix...the physics?"

He was surely speaking non-literally. Alice remembered a particularly sarcastic first officer who—in the middle of a war—would say things like, "barring some change in the laws of physics, this next torpedo will be a direct hit; brace for impact." Captain Hadder's delivery was wanting, but she felt certain that he was aiming for the same sort of droll wit.

"They're not *broken*, they're *wrong*," he said. "I'm amazed you've survived on board the ship for this long, corporal."

"I haven't...Captain. Just tell me where the rest of the crew is, and I'll go find someone who can help."

"As I said, they could be in their quarters. Computer, are the crew in their quarters?"

"The crew may or may not be in quarters, captain."

"There, see?" he said. "They may be there."

"Then should we go down and check?" she asked. "I passed the quarters on my way."

"Oh, goodness no, don't do that. Imagine the consequences."

"I don't understand."

"Corporal, it's really very simple. I don't know if they're alive or not. If I check, I will *definitely* know. Who wants that on their conscience?"

"They're either alive or they're not alive," Alice said.

"The computer confirmed, they are both. Have you ever seen a person who was both alive and dead?"

"Of course not. Those are binary states."

"Neither have I. Therefore, if they are currently both alive *and* dead, and one of us were to go down to see which one it was, and *we* have never seen a person who was both alive and dead, then by checking, we will ensure that they are either one or the other, and I want no part of that! Neither should you, after what happened to poor Ensign Anson. Already enough blood on *your* hands."

About ninety-five percent of Alice thought this was the most ridiculous thing she'd ever heard. The five percent that didn't was the same five percent that was in charge when she ran down the corridor in deck five, in the midst of something like a panic attack. She didn't want to open those doors either, even before having her intelligence assaulted by Captain Hadder's nonsense.

"How about if we just open a comm line, right now?" she asked. "We can hail the *Rosen*."

"Oh no, that's impossible. Nothing on the bridge works right now."

She looked around. The panels were lit, which wasn't an expectation on a non-working bridge.

"You have power. It all looks like it's working."

"It's not," he said. "Hasn't been since yesterday. And even though we clearly *do* have power, the engine isn't providing it. Couldn't tell you what is."

She pointed to one of the chairs at the front of the deck. "May I?" she asked.

Captain Hadder stepped aside and waved her through.

She sat down at what was—if she remembered the ship design specs accurately—the helmsman's chair. It had all the navigational instrumentation, and the communications matrix.

All the ships in the USF communicated locally by sending concentrated radioelectric bursts in tight, targeted beams. A similar approach was used for long-range communications, only the local transmission was sent to a relay, which repeated the information through an FTL tunnel.

The *Rosen* was just at the edge of Quadrant Brenda. In a rational universe, the *Erwin* would already know the *Rosen* was there, either because the *Rosen* pinged it when it was in range—which it did, as part of the ongoing effort to establish communication—or because the mid-range sensors have only one job, which is to detect nearby objects and keep track of them.

Possibly, the *Erwin* was no longer a participant in a rational universe.

She asked the ship to perform a full sensor sweep, and while there was some good news—it *did* pick up the *Rosen*, and her shuttle—according to the survey, there was *nothing* on the starboard side.

Not just *nothing*, as in, *space is pretty much a lot of nothing anyway* nothing. This was a nothingness that far exceeded any previously recorded nothing, on a scale that made it quite a remarkable something. There were no quantum fluctuations popping in virtual particles, or the evidence of gravitational force acting at a distance to warp the fabric of spacetime, or microscopic space debris. There were no solar winds. There was just nothing.

Alice was reminded of the ancient Earth maps: those two-dimensional rectangles meant to approximate a portion of a spherical object. The early ones weren't large enough to encompass the entire planet, so when one drew a line to the edge of the map, it wasn't an expectation that the line would pick up again on the opposite side. There was nothing else there because the mapmaker had stopped drawing what came next.

This is the end of the map, she thought. *Here be dragons.*

"No, that can't be right," she said. "It must be a sensor malfunction."

"Sensors operating at full capacity," the computer said, helpfully.

Alice stood up and leaned, to get a look at that side of the ship. If she didn't know better, she'd have said someone was out there, hanging a gigantic piece of non-reflective fabric over that part of space. Maybe they were.

"Oh no, don't do that," Hadder said.

"Do what?"

"*Stare* at the Void. Never a good idea,"

"You know about this?"

"Of course I do. It's why the ship isn't moving."

"Great, now we're getting somewhere. Tell me what it is, and then maybe we can work up a strategy to get away from it."

"It's nothing. You read the sensors. I don't know why you're acting so surprised, I *told* you what the problem was already."

"You didn't mention the giant Void in space," she said. "I would have remembered that."

"I said *nothing* was the matter with the ship. That's very clear."

She sighed, and resisted the urge to draw her blaster again."

"Doesn't matter," she said. "I can still see the *Rosen*. I'll hail them, set up a tow."

"Best of luck!"

She opened a channel.

"USF *Rosen*, this is Corporal Aste, on the USF *Erwin*. Please respond."

The transmission came from the radar array at the highest point on the top of the *Erwin*, with secondary and tertiary arrays on the underbelly, in the event of damage from space debris or an act of violence. When Alice sent the transmission, the signal was transmitted by all three.

Alice already knew this was how local communication worked, but this time she got a dramatic demonstration of it, because for some reason the radio signal she sent out became visible for five full seconds, before falling apart.

It was hard to get a total count on the number of things that was wrong with this. Radio waves weren't supposed to be a part of the visible spectrum, so that was a big problem right there. Also, before the signals dissolved (or whatever that was) those beams of impossible-but-true visible light *slowed down*.

Alice checked the communications array to confirm that the frequency she chose to send the signal on was a normal, non-visible-spectrum frequency. It was.

"Don't try the laser," Hadder said. He meant the high-burst pulse communicator, which was meant for long-range emergency signaling. "Unless you dislike the *Rosen*."

"You tried it already?"

"It was like birthing a sun. Very beautiful! Given its speed and direction, I'm afraid that beam may be well on its way to annihilating everyone who lives in the Podolsky System. First Officer Hart worked that out."

This was the first time Hadder mentioned a member of the bridge crew other than the departed Ensign Anson. She thought that was a significant thing.

"First Officer Regina Hart?" she said. "Where is she now? In her quarters?"

"I'm afraid not. She's left."

"L...left. Left the bridge? Left the ship?"

"She's in the Anthropene Principality now. I'll see her soon, I'm sure."

"Where is that?" Alice asked. It wasn't a place she'd ever heard of before. Not that it mattered if she *had*; it was impossible to walk off a ship in deep space and visit much of anywhere, and there was a full complement of shuttles in the hangar. Wherever it was, First Officer Hart wasn't actually there.

Hadder laughed, and gestured vaguely at the expanse of space. *Oh, you know*, the gesture said. *Let's not be silly*.

Exasperated, Alice sat back down in the helm chair and rubbed her head. She could feel a headache coming on.

"I wonder," she said, "If one of you—captain or computer—can tell me what actually happened, or why, or even when?"

Hadder laughed again.

"Why, I'm not sure!" he said. "What an excellent question. I know what we can do. Computer?"

"Yes captain," the computer said.

"Switch to narrative mode."

"Narrative mode?" Alice asked. "That's not even..."

The computer began speaking again, only this time in a deeper voice that wasn't precisely the same as the sing-songy soothing one all the USF ships were stuck with.

"Things began to go badly for the crew of the United Space Fleet science vessel Erwin around the time Dr. Marchere's coffee mug spontaneously reassembled itself.

Dr. Louis Marchere was not, at that moment, conducting some manner of experiment. Well, he was, only not on entropy and the nature of time. He was running several other tests, of the kind that make perfect sense on a scientific vessel such as the Erwin. About half of them were biological in nature, concerning how small samples of cellular material reacts to certain deep space factors. Other tests were more at home in the general field of astrophysics. But—again, as this is important—he was not conducting a test on entropy."

"Computer, stop," *Hadder said.* "There, that was helpful, wasn't it?"

"What the hell was that?" *Alice asked.* "And why is the computer doing that?"

"Doing what?"

"It said *Alice said,* when I was talking, and the same thing when you were talking."

"It's narrative mode. Useful! Now we know it all began with Dr. Marchere."

Alice was deeply confused. She'd never heard of narrative

mode before, and was nearly positive Hadder was playing some sort of elaborate joke.

"It's not a *joke!*" Hadder said.

"I didn't say it was!"

"The *narrative* did."

"Turn it off," *Alice said.* "I KNOW I SAID THAT, YOU DON'T HAVE TO TELL ME I SAID THAT."

"Computer, end narrative mode."

"Ending narrative mode," the computer said.

"Oh, thank God," she said. "All right, so, Dr. Louis Marchere. Where is he? Or did he go to the...whatever-you-said place?"

"No, I believe he's still on-board," Hadder said. "We were just speaking. Deck three, in the research lab."

"Great. Let's go."

She headed for the elevator. Hadder remained where he was.

"Well, come on," she said. "You're the only survivor I've found so far; I think we should stick together, don't you?"

"It's...um, no. No, I think my place is on the bridge," he said. "It's safer."

"Captain Hadder, I don't think any part of this ship is safe. Our best option here is to find out what Marchere knows; if he doesn't have a way to save the *Erwin*, we need to get to my shuttle."

"Find out what you can," he said, in a tone that sounded like an order, "and keep me updated! Much to do up here."

He sat down in the captain's chair, as if this settled things.

"All right," she said. "I'll, ah, I'll let you know. Computer, deck three."

"Deck three," the computer confirmed.

As the doors closed, Alice could have sworn she saw Ensign Anson standing next to Captain Hadder.

But of course, she didn't. That would be impossible.

***

IT TOOK TWICE AS LONG to get to the third deck from the first as it did to get to the first deck from the fifth. Alice was quite certain there was no mechanism in existence capable of adding fractional decks to the ship, and so was chalking this up to another aspect of the ongoing computer malfunction. She supposed a way to validate this was to ask that the elevator stop at, say, deck two-and-five-sixteenths, but she also didn't want to encourage the computer's departures from reality any more than necessary.

Find the problem, she thought. *Find the problem, work the problem, solve the problem.*

The reason Corporal Alice Aste was an ideal rescue mission envoy was that, over the course of a fairly extensive career, she'd worked in just about every part of a starship, from engine to helm. She was a problem-solving universal tool, a one-person away team. If a disabled ship was disabled because there was nobody on-board with the expertise to re-enable the vessel, the likelihood was fairly high that Alice had the gap-filling skillset.

But this? Whatever was going on aboard the USF *Erwin,* she wasn't equipped to deal with it. Maybe nobody human was.

"The subjective mind is objectively flawed," she said aloud. It was one of the philosophical-slash-practical mottos she lived by. She couldn't recall who said it to her originally—probably one of her academy professors—but she'd found it incredibly useful over the years. There were some things the human mind was simply bad at grasping, observationally or intuitively, which was why flawed humans created machines to objectively interrogate the world for them.

That was what the computer was supposed to be doing.

Since it was malfunctioning, Alice had no way to determine how much of what she was experiencing was even *real*.

And that was terrifying.

"Deck three," the computer announced, finally.

The door slid open, revealing a corridor with glass-walled rooms on both sides.

Scientific research was the *Erwin's* central function, which was why the third deck was its widest and tallest. (Looked at from the front, the *Erwin* looked like a wide oval or, if you were hungry, like an overstuffed sandwich; deck three was where all the meat was located.) It was also where most of the vessel's funding went.

There was a dizzying amount of experimentational activity taking place in both of the glassed-in rooms, nearly all of it mechanized. If quizzed, Alice could definitively identify maybe a third of the experiments, and perhaps half of the equipment.

The ship's supercollider—one of only a half-dozen off-planet supercolliders in existence—was running some kind of test on the far wall on her left, while on the right a laser tube designed to detect gravitational waves was humming along. A little further along, a hologram of a Moebius strip was rotating slowly, beside a bank of computer screens displaying rapidly evolving fractals.

Those were just the most obvious, macroscopic things. There were also cultured cell somewhere, having things done to them, and top secret genetic splicing research, and plants being taught to grow in zero gravity chambers, and much more, but she couldn't see any of that.

She kept walking down the corridor, absorbing the maelstrom of activity on both sides, wondering exactly where all the power for this was coming from. The supercollider alone was supposed to take up enough of the energy from the *Erwin's* fusion engine that the vessel couldn't run the FTL drive as long as it was also going. (This was not a safety precaution, although it may as well have been. Nobody was sure what would happen if a supercollider ran while on a ship traveling faster-than-light-speed, but the consensus was: nothing good.)

The point was, everything running *at once* had to be an enormous drain, and yet the captain insisted the ship's engine wasn't even running. Either he was wrong—he was crazy, so it was probably that—or the *Erwin* was surviving on battery power. The batteries on a ship like this supplied just about enough power to keep life support going, plus the communications array, and *maybe* some impulse power for basic maneuverability, for about thirty days. It couldn't do all that and also provide a city's worth of energy to the research deck.

And yet, that appeared to be what was happening. Unless Hadder was wrong.

"Computer," she said, "give me a read on the ship's engine output?"

"The engine is not running," the computer said.

"Not the propulsion. I know we aren't moving. The base-level output."

"The engine is not running."

"Computer, the ship has power, does it not? Otherwise, you and I wouldn't be talking and I wouldn't be able to breathe."

"Confirmed, the ship has power."

"Then what's the engine's baseline output?"

"The engine is not running."

"Fine," Alice said. "Computer, what is the source of the ship's power, if not the engine? Is it the auxiliary batteries, or something else?"

"What is the answer you are expecting?" the computer asked.

"The right answer would be great."

"The batteries are providing the ship with power."

"Did you just say that because you thought that was what I wanted to hear?"

"The batteries are providing the ship with power."

"Sure."

"Would you like to switch to narrative mode?"

"No. What is it with you and narrative mode?"

"Narrative mode has been proven to reveal information not otherwise available to this computer."

"No, thank you."

She stopped short of asking the computer what other modes it had available, both because this was yet another ridiculous conversation she had no time for, and because she could see someone moving in the last part of the lab on the right.

The man had on a lead vest, with goggles and a face shield dangling loosely around his neck. He was also wearing thick leather gloves, brown coveralls of the sort Alice recognized as standard for the engineers, and heavy mag-spiked boots. His hair was pointed in five different directions, and he was holding something that looked like a blowtorch in one hand.

He could have been just about anyone in the crew. Nonetheless, she felt certain that this was Dr. Marchere.

Alice walked up to the nearest door, and when it wouldn't open, tried her override code. That didn't work either, so she knocked.

She startled him; he nearly dropped the torch, which would have been very bad had it been lit.

"Dr. Marchere?" she shouted.

He waved, put down the torch, waddled over, and opened the door.

"Very sorry, I'm extremely busy, can you come back later?" he asked.

"I really can't," she said. "I'm here to rescue the ship."

"I...see. And you are?"

"Corporal Alice Aste. I'm with the Security Force, and—"

"All right, all right, come in. Rescue! Ha-ha. Yes. That would be *something*."

She stepped into the room, which was awash in an atonal cacophony of pings, whirrs, and clangs. He took off his gloves and led her to a table in the center of all of it. On the table was a coffee mug, a cold pot of coffee, and a plate of doughnuts.

"I would offer you something other than doughnuts," he said, "but the food replicator can only make these, and only if one asks for bicarbonate of soda. I haven't worked out what one is supposed to request in order to get other foods, so this is what I have. Now, you've exactly seventeen minutes, and then I'll have to get back. I'm running thirty-eight experiments, and as you can see all of my colleagues have already left."

"Where did they go?"

"They left, as I said. You're not from the *Erwin*, is that right?"

"The *Rosen* is nearby. If we can't get the *Erwin's* engine running, we'll have to get the *Rosen* here for a tow. I can't hail them for...some reason, but I can try calling them from my shuttle. I just need to understand what's happening here, first. The computer...I'm sorry, this will sound insane, but in narrative mode, whatever that is, the computer said that this all began when Dr. Louis Marchere dropped a coffee mug. You *are* Dr. Louis Marchere, aren't you?"

"I am! And that is *amazing*."

"Which part?"

"All of it! I'm amazed you've lasted this long. Have you come across anyone else?"

"The captain and I had a long conversation that made no sense and confused everything much more."

"Oh, excellent, the captain is still here. I was sure I was the last one left."

"He said he thinks the crew might be in their quarters, but is afraid to check, because he thinks if he does so, they might be dead and it will be his fault." She laughed then, to see if Marchere was inspired to laugh as well. He was not.

"Yes, that's eminently reasonable on his part," he said. "Narrative mode, you say? That's a new one. I accidentally stumbled upon theatrical mode yesterday, which was odd enough."

"Switching to theatrical mode," the computer said.

Marchere: No, I didn't mean for that. Oh well, here we are. Welcome to theatrical mode.

Alice: Oh, this is very strange.

Marchere: Yes well, now we're here. It's not *terrible*. I enjoyed it during a soliloquy, but after became quite frustrated.

(*Marchere takes a bite of a doughnut.*)

Marchere: There, you see, it's exhausting, having your own actions read back to you. I became obsessed with the question of whether the computer was describing what I was doing, or if I was doing what the computer instructed me to do. Did I just bite this doughnut because that was what the stage business described, or did the stage business capture my actions?

(*Alice looks confused.*)

Alice: Weird, it's in present-tense. And the computer keeps announcing who's speaking, like we don't already know. It was doing that before too, in narrative mode, only not every time.

Marchere: The fact that it's *in* present-tense is what makes it so confounding. That would argue in favor of it dictating my actions instead of the other way around, which would contravene the concept of free will *entirely*, and that's terribly frustrating.

Alice: I shot a man on the bridge before pulling the trigger on my blaster. Captain Hadder said it was because cause-and-effect had been malfunctioning all day. That sounds like a similar problem. Can we...turn this off?

Marchere: Computer, end theatrical mode.

"Ending theatrical mode," the computer said.

"Thank you," Alice said. "Now can you *please* explain what's happened here? Where did everyone go, why are you running all of these experiments, where are you even getting the *power* to run all of these experiments?"

"Do you want for me to answer all of those at the same time, or is there a particular order you'd like for me to honor?"

"Start with what's going on. I guess."

"All right. Do you know what scientific theory states that the laws of physics are the same everywhere?"

"No, I don't."

"Good, because there isn't one. We've always just assumed it to be so, because it did us no good to assume otherwise. It was a poor assumption."

"You're saying the laws of physics don't apply to this quadrant?"

"I mean the Void we're next to, primarily, but as you must have worked out, there have been local alterations. We're right on the event horizon of a portion of space in which nothing we've previously proven to be true is *necessarily* still true. That's why I'm running all these experiments. I'm trying to work out what *is* true in this particular region of space."

"That sounds ridiculous."

"Oh, absolutely. It's magnificently ridiculous. Yesterday, I positively identified a particle's exact location *and* velocity. This morning, I tested the wave function collapse of light, but it refused to collapse. Later, I managed to measure the speed of light from a moving object compared to the speed of light from a stationary one, and discovered the one from the moving object was *faster*. I've also discovered electrons a *half-quanta* apart, and a few hours ago the supercollider detected an element between carbon and nitrogen, and a neutron with a negative charge. And this morning, for five seconds, all the oxygen in the other room—thankfully, I was in this one—gathered in one corner. These are all impossible, ridiculous things."

"But that can't be right. It's only a computer malfunction."

"The computer on this ship is working perfectly," he said, "in that it's describing an objective reality we cannot grasp. My equipment is working perfectly as well. It's our perception that's having trouble catching up. Now, I have to get back to my work before it's too late."

"Too late for what, doctor?" she asked. "What *exactly* happened to your coworkers? Where is everyone else?"

"Ah. They don't exist any longer."

"You mean, they're dead?"

"I prefer it the way I said it. Are you familiar with the anthropic principle?"

"I heard...something *like* that. The captain said his bridge crew went to the Anthropene Principality. Is that the same thing?"

"More or less. Hadder's head's all jumbled. The anthropic principle is a logical point stemming from the observation that everything in our universe has to be *just so*, in order to allow for our existence. From Planck's Constant to the charge of an electron, the weight of atomic particles, and so on and so forth, all of it carries a value which allows, as an aggregate, for a universe to exist which contains intelligent life. None of these values *had* to be what they were. It's a little circular, because one could easily argue that the only reason the universe's aggregation of values exists to allow intelligent life is because this is the only permutation that allowed for intelligent life to develop in order to make that observation. Other universes—assuming multiple universes —evolved differently, and have no intelligent life to note that their universe failed to evolve in such a way to allow for them to exist."

"All right," she said. "That does sound odd."

"I bring it up because the part of the universe we're standing at the edge of, right now, is a part where the laws do *not* allow for us to exist. It's the converse point of the anthropic principle. We're composed of the laws on which our universe was built. The slightest change in the strong nuclear charge, and the atoms that make up your body could fly apart or collapse into themselves. Your brain evolved to communicate via neural electrical charges; a change in the electromagnetic force, and it stops working. These are facile examples, but you understand. If the laws change, we won't be around to measure them. At least, not for long. We're still *here* because neither of us have had the misfortune to happen upon a patch of altered laws that will undo us, and in fact right now we're *alive* because I've been taking advantage of the alteration. You asked before what's powering us. The answer is, when the engine failed, I hooked up the auxiliary batteries to one another. They're now charging one another *and* the ship."

"That's impossible."

"Evidently not here! The laws of this patch of universe allow for perpetual motion machines, so we may as well get some use out of it."

"So...you're saying the rest of the crew has been...unmade?"

"I've yet to witness this happening to anyone, but yes, I think so. I'm afraid to leave this level. You say you came from the hangar, and visited the bridge; it's good to know those places still exist."

"According to the computer, there are fractional decks being added all the time," she said.

He laughed.

"Fascinating," he said. "I only hope I'm around to find an explanation for *that*."

"Now that I'm here with a shuttle, you don't have to think

like that, doctor," she said. "I can take you—and the captain, if he's willing to leave the bridge—and whatever research you have. The *Erwin* is clearly a hostile living environment."

"An excellent suggestion, but no, I think I had better stay. You have a good point, however, in that I have no way to communicate my findings. My hope was to record as much as I could and jettison it toward the hub, but in truth I came upon that idea when I thought I'd reach the *end* of my studies. It seems the deeper I dig, the more strangeness I find. But here."

He placed a memory tab on the table.

This is everything I've measured up to about an hour ago. I hope."

"You hope?"

"I hope it's only been an hour. The passage of time has been curious."

She picked up the tab.

"It has," she said, "the captain said it had only been a day, but it's been..."

Alice looked up from the table to find she was speaking to an empty room.

"Dr. Marchere?"

He'd been standing five feet away, and now he wasn't. The experiments in the room were still running, and the doughnut he'd taken a bite from remained bitten from, but he wasn't there to continue the experiments or finish the doughnut.

"Computer, can you locate Dr. Marchere?"

"There is no Dr. Marchere."

"Dr. Louis Marchere," she clarified.

"There is no Dr. Louis Marchere."

"He was just right here, computer."

"Would you like to try a different narration?"

"No, I...I don't know what I want."

He's in the Anthropene Principality now, she thought.

"I need to get off this ship," she decided. "Computer, what's the fastest way to the hangar?"

"The hangar is located on deck five," the computer said.

"Is there still a deck five?"

"There's still a deck five, but portions appear missing. Haste is recommended."

Alice opened the door to the lab and ran to the elevator, as things in both glass-walled rooms began to go somewhat *more* haywire than before. The holographic Moebius strip had developed a second side, the fractals on the computer screens began flashing random Greek letters for some reason, and it looked like a black hole was forming in the center of the supercollider. An amoeba the size of her head popped into existence on the glass a few feet from her face, and then popped back out of existence again before she had a chance to scream. It began to rain.

She reached the elevator door and pushed the button. Then she opened up her bag and retrieved her helmet. If the atmosphere decided to collect in one corner of the ship again, she'd rather she was breathing her own supply.

The ship started groaning before the elevator even made it to the fourth deck.

"Computer, what made that sound?" Alice asked.

"Unclear."

Alice remembered visiting the extinct-Earth-animals exhibit as a child, and being transfixed by the elephant in particular. The noises the ship was making sounded like an elephant being squeezed like an exhaust bladder.

Then the elevator shuddered, and stopped.

"Computer, what's going on?"

"Unclear."

"Can you tell me where I've stopped?"

"You've stopped at deck three-and-eleven-sixteenths. Would you like to get out here?"

"That depends. Will the elevator be moving again any time soon?"

"Define *soon*."

"Before the ship blows up, implodes, or otherwise ceases to exist?"

"Unable to predict those outcomes at this time."

Alice wondered if maybe she should have gone up instead, back to the bridge. She could have collected Captain Hadder and gone out the topside hatch, and called the shuttle from there.

Then Alice started floating: the gravity had cut out.

If I can get into the shaft, I can reach the command deck on my own, she thought.

"Computer, can you hail Captain Hadder?" she asked.

"There is no Captain Hadder."

"Computer, can you hail the bridge?"

"There is no bridge."

"Deck one, computer. Open a channel to deck one."

"There is no deck one."

Crap.

"Computer, does deck five still exist?"

"Deck five continues to exist."

"But deck one is missing."

"The USF *Erwin* does not have a deck one."

"All right, never mind. Open doors, please. Let's see what deck three-and-eleven-sixteenths looks like."

The doors slid open on a level that looked weirdly out-of-focus. Alice's first thought was that some kind of viscous fluid had gotten on her helmet, distorting the view of the universe on the other side. But the helmet was clean.

The walls were partly transparent and partly solid, because deck four's walls were opaque, while deck three's floors had glass walls. Deck three-and-eleven-sixteenths was trying to have both at once.

Since the gravity was out, Alice activated the mag-spikes on her boots and attached herself to the floor, then stepped off the elevator onto a blurry level that somehow managed to be solid.

"Computer, where is the nearest maintenance shaft on this deck?" she asked.

If the ship behaved for long enough, she'd be able to access the fifth deck by way of a maintenance shaft.

"Twenty-five meters."

"In which direction?"

"All directions."

The computer was not going to help.

Relying on the deck layout of one of the levels that was actually supposed to exist, Alice headed straight down the blurry corridor between the blurry rooms on both sides. In a slightly more ideal circumstance, she'd run, but because the artificial gravity generator had decided it was done (or ceased to exist, or whatever), she had to keep one boot on the ground.

About fifteen steps in, the boots stopped working. Actually, what it felt like was that the magnets holding her in place switched poles spontaneously, and repelled her from the floor. She began drifting to the ceiling.

Then came an explosion, somewhere aboard the ship. Alice felt it tremble through the belly of the vessel, rocking the walls, and putting her into a gentle spin.

"Computer, what was that?"

"That was an explosion," the computer said, not at all helpfully.

"Right, thanks."

There was another tremble, and a shudder, and then a loud screech that didn't sound like much of anything Alice had ever heard before: not the noise a machine makes when it's broken, or a sound approximating that of an extinct elephant getting squeezed, or the cacophony a ship makes when its hull is torn open. It was not, in other words, on the short list of *bad noises* in her mental catalog of things to be alarmed about. She was, nevertheless, extremely alarmed, because what it *did* sound like, was a creature that her lizard brain told her to run from. This was even though that portion of her brain *also* didn't know what she was hearing.

Then, directly beneath her and along the corridor floor, a *thing* ran past.

There were a tremendous number of wrong things that were wrong with this thing, the most arresting being that it was somehow in a higher definition than the rest of the deck, including Alice herself. It was a bright shade of blue, and green, almond, and a color of purple she was pretty sure was ultraviolet, which she was also pretty sure she shouldn't have been able to see. There were other colors she didn't even have a name for, because they didn't exist in the universe she was familiar with.

It was perhaps a giant bat, perhaps a snake, and perhaps a horse. It galloped and hissed, shrieked and chortled, and swung its long, clawed fingers through the walls on either side as if they weren't there. The walls, in turn, acted as if the creature wasn't there, showing no damage.

Here be dragons, she thought.

With a great flap of its enormous wings, it soared ahead, and vanished at the far end of the corridor.

"All right, I've had enough," Alice said. "Computer what's the fastest way off this ship? I don't care *how*, just as long as it puts me on the other side of the hull."

"Unable to calculate," the computer said.

"Why is that?"

"The concept of *other side of the hull* is too variable to allow for a precise calculation. There are several places where the hull has ceased to exist, but sensors indicate nothing exists on the other side of where the hull no longer is."

"That's great."

The vessel shuddered again. Alice waited for a new nightmare creature to show up, but none did. It was probably just another part of the *Erwin* getting unwritten from the universe.

"Computer, how close am I to the maintenance shaft now?"

"Twenty-five meters."

"That's how far I was when I got off the broken elevator. I must have gotten closer since."

"Understood. However, the distance remains twenty-five meters."

She sighed.

"I really need to understand what's happening to the entire ship right now, computer," Alice said. "Or I'm never getting off of it. I don't even know what questions to ask you. Can you provide me with an integrity assessment?"

"Not in this mode."

A hole opened up in the floor, which should have been good news, because that was the direction she wanted to go. But there was nothing on the other side of the hole. Either decks four and five were missing now, or the hole just went to someplace different.

"What the hell," Alice said. "Computer, switch to narrative mode."

SOMETHING *quite extraordinary was happening to the USF Erwin.*

It was difficult to tell, from more or less any angle, whether the ship had been drawing closer to the Void on its starboard, or if the Void was moving closer to the ship, but what was definitely the case was that their positions relative to one another had been changing since the Erwin first encountered the strange section of space. Now—after either two days or six weeks—the two things were colliding.

The Void was having a devastating effect on the Erwin. (The same could not be said of the Erwin's impact on the Void, which appeared to be weathering things just fine.) There were certain expectations regarding how most space-based threats could damage a manmade starship. Incredibly dense objects, like neutron stars or black holes, could tear apart such a ship if it ventured too close, by literally ripping parts of the vessel off of other parts of the vessel, and/or drawing it into an inescapable gravitational well. Highly radioactive objects could bombard the ship with levels of gamma radiation so severe as to overwhelm the shielding and cook whoever is unfortunate enough to be inside. Rogue objects like asteroids could blow through a hull with a direct hit.

And so on.

None of those things were happening to the Erwin. Instead, it looked as if someone had produced a very realistic three-dimensional artistic rendering of the ship, and then, deciding they disliked it, began erasing the artwork. Starting on the starboard side, large chunks of solid material were being turned into tiny bits of particulate matter—eraser crumbs, perhaps—after which the tiny bits of particulate matter glistened with internal light, and then vanished.

It's fair to say that however beautiful this might have looked to a neutral (and presumably distant) observer, its impact on the contents of the vessel was very bad indeed. Under optimal circumstances, a hull breach was dealt with by the ship's integrity shields: short-term force fields that plugged up holes before all of the atmosphere in the breached cell leaked into space. But the integrity shields only worked in circumstances where there was more hull than breach, and anyway they needed power in order to function. Unfortunately, the entirely impossible perpetual motion machine Dr. Marchere assembled had begun to break down.

All of this would be very bad news for anyone still alive aboard the USF Erwin. It was good news, then—if such a thing deserved to be called good news, that there was nobody left alive on the Erwin. All except for Corporal Alice Aste, desperately shuffling along deck three-and-eleven-sixteenths in a quixotic attempt to get back to her shuttle before she too was unmade, like the others.

"Hey!" *Alice said.* "There's no need for that."

The deck floor was mostly gone now, as was the starboard side of the hull, which she could see through the blurry office wall: the Void was on two sides. The ceiling remained intact, though, and since there was no such thing as up or down in space —especially without the artificial gravity—she was doing okay with her mag-spiked boots. Shortly, though, she was going to run out of places to move.

"Computer, if you could just stop being so long-winded and give me something I can use, that would be great," *she said.*

"The nature and pace of the narrative isn't under the computer's control," *the computer said, annoyingly.*

Alice grumbled an insult under her breath, and kept going. Very shortly, none of this would matter. Already, the port side hull was weakening, not so much from direct contact with the void, but as a consequence of having its structural integrity challenged thanks to half of it no longer existing. The hull's metal shell was wrinkling...

"Hang on, go back," *Alice said.* "Repeat that last part."

Alice grumbled an insult...

"After that."

Already, the port side hull was weakening...

"COMPUTER, END NARRATIVE MODE."

"Ending narrative mode."

Alice put her hand on the blurry med lab wall on the port side. It felt firm under her hands, because it was a wall, but at the same time it also didn't feel *that* firm. She pushed...and her hand went through it.

"Okay, that probably shouldn't have worked," she said.

She kicked her leg through, and then her other arm, and soon she'd gotten her whole body on the other side. Now in a room that was trying very hard to be both Marchere's supercollider lab and a medical examination room, she mag-walked across the ceiling to the outer hull.

The pushing-her-hand-through-something-that-was-supposed-to-be-solid trick didn't work a second time; the hull was firm, although she could hear it starting to fail. Waiting for that to happen seemed like a bad bet, and she didn't have to; not as long as she was carrying explosive charges.

She pulled one out, set the digital timer to thirty seconds, said a quiet prayer that she was in a part of the ship where chemical explosives and digital clocks still worked like they were supposed to, and then disengaged the mag-clips from the ceiling and pushed herself to the far end of the room.

The charge went off, exposing all of deck three-and-eleven-sixteenths to outer space. The atmosphere blew out of the hole, and sucked Alice out with it. In seconds, she was drifting on a free trajectory a significant distance from the Erwin.

"Now unsynchronized with USF Erwin's computer," her suit's computer announced, which Alice thought was great news.

"Call the shuttle to my position," Alice said.

"Unable to locate shuttle," the computer said.

Alice twisted around until she was facing the wreckage of the *Erwin*. She could see the shuttle all right, but it was now embedded in the side of the larger ship. It looked like the *Erwin* was giving birth to it, only in reverse.

"That's great," she said.

The Void was just about done with the *Erwin*. Like the narrative said, it was hard to tell whether the ship had been drifting into the Void or whether the Void was expanding to consume the ship. Either way, she couldn't afford to drift into it herself, nor could she ask the *Rosen* to get that close to it just to pick her up.

But, she wasn't out of options. There were two more charges in her bag, and the bag had armor shielding.

She pulled it off her back and got out the two remaining charges.

"Computer, locate the *Rosen*," she said. Then she held her breath. If the computer said *unable to locate* or worse, *the USF Rosen does not exist*, Alice was out of luck. It said neither.

"*Rosen* located."

"Target on helmet view."

The computer pinpointed the ship for her.

Now's the fun part, she thought. She set the timer for both charges at thirty seconds, put them back in the bag, and then tried to crouch until her whole body—feet-first so her legs would absorb the worst of it—was behind the steel plate in the bag. Then she tried to maneuver herself so that she was between the impending explosion and the USF *Rosen*.

"Computer, activate emergency beacon," she said.

"Emergency beacon activated."

"Thanks. Sure hope this works."

The charges blew. She felt her right leg shatter, and then she blacked out.

SHE WOKE up in the *Rosen's* med-lab, with a doctor she didn't know standing over her.

"There you are," he said. "Welcome back."

"Thanks," she said. Her mouth was dry and her vision blurry.

How long have I been out? she wondered.

She tried to sit up, but it felt like the *Rosen's* gravity was set at a much higher force level than it was supposed to be.

"Here, let me help," the doctor said, pushing a button that got her bed into an upright position. "I'm Dr. Maxwell, and you are lucky to be alive."

"You wouldn't be the first doctor to tell me that," she said, trying out a smile. "What's the damage?"

"Broken right leg, shattered left kneecap, broken left elbow, torn muscles in your right shoulder, and your oxygen ran out three minutes before we got to you, so you're probably missing a few brain cells. There were a couple of other things, but that's the worst of it."

"I need to speak to the captain," she said.

"Oh, I'm sure. I'll let him know you're awake; he'll want to speak to you too. They've been going over the information you retrieved from the *Erwin*; I guess there are a lot of questions they need answering."

"How long...?"

"How long have you been out?" he asked. "Depends on where you'd like to start counting. We believe you were adrift for a couple of days, but you'd been on board the *Erwin* for more than a week. Your trip computer recorded only a few hours, though. I think this is one of the questions the captain has. You *do* need some rest first, so if you'd like for me to delay him, I can certainly do so."

"No," she said. "It's okay. The sooner the better."

"Good," he said, with a paternal smile. "I'll let him know. Meanwhile, if you're thirsty, there's a glass of water on your right. I'll be right back."

He left. Alice sat still for a few minutes, trying to compose her thoughts. It was going to be impossible to explain everything without sounding insane, but she didn't really care about coming off as sane any more. What happened, happened. They'll have to take the data from Dr. Marchere, and her accounting, and figure out what to do with it. Hopefully, one of the things they would decide to do would be to bar all travel through Quadrant Brenda.

After a few minutes with her thoughts, Alice realized she was fantastically thirsty. She turned and reached for the glass, not entirely anticipating how weak her right arm was. What began as a straightforward reach for a nearby object became an awkward flail that resulted in her knocking the glass off the edge of the counter.

She heard it shatter on the floor.

"Great," she said. "You gave me an actual glass. Very smart, Dr. Maxwell."

Alice was deciding whether to call a nurse to clean up the glass or to try and do it herself—despite the cast on her leg—when the drinking glass reassembled itself and returned to the counter.

She blinked a couple of times, thinking it would be best if she pretended that hadn't just happened, while knowing that pretending this wouldn't make a difference.

"Computer," she said.

"Yes, Corporal Aste," the *Rosen's* computer said.

"This is going to sound like crazy, but do you have a narrative mode?"

PRIMORDIAL SOUP AND SALAD

Wallace Englund, captain of the United Space Fleet vessel *Caroline*, stared out his private office window at the only view he'd had for nearly four years—outer space, in all its dull glory—and wondered why he couldn't get a decent cheeseburger.

Behind him were the last three attempts at a burger, made by the ship's food replicator. The first looked okay, until Wallace bit into it and discovered a soft, gelatinous interior that still *tasted* like a cheeseburger but whose texture made it impossible to ingest. The second was visibly worse: the left side of the burger looked like brown gravy, and not in a good way. The third came out perfect, up until Wallace touched the top of the bun at which time it collapsed into a thick, lumpy puddle.

Now lined up on his conference table like a surrealist *Descent of Man*, the indigestible catastrophes awaited an explanation from someone who knew how to tame a misbehaving food replicator.

The sensor above the door whistled.

"Enter," the captain said, and in walked his ship's chief engineer. "There you are, Tandy. What took you?"

Chief Engineer Tandy McKinnon looked tired. But, she *always* looked tired.

"I don't think the ship wants to make it to port," she said. "Or if she does, she'd rather we weren't alive for the experience. That's my guess."

"Anything critical?"

"Semi-critical. We lost life support on deck three for a minute and a half but nobody had to hold their breath or anything. Didn't even notice until the dioxide scrubbers sounded an alarm. You want a full accounting?"

"Save it for the end-of-shift report," he said.

Tandy looked at the parade of misbegotten cheeseburgers. "What's this?" she asked.

"*This* is what happened when I tried to order lunch."

She leaned over to get a better look. "Huh. How'd it taste?"

"That's not the point."

"Maybe you should ask for a cheeseburger soup, see what happens."

"Tandy," he said, exasperated at her degree of levity. "Self-evidently something is amiss with the food replicator."

"Computer," Tandy said, "are the food replicators working?"

"The food replicators are functioning within normal parameters, Chief Engineer McKinnon," the computer said, in its usual annoyingly cheerful voice.

"*She* doesn't think there's anything wrong with them," Tandy said.

"Yes, well the computer doesn't eat. Do you, computer?"

"You are correct, Captain Englund, the computer does not eat."

"Come on, Tandy, what's going on?"

Tandy walked over to the replicator station built into the

wall and ordered a glass of water. She sat back down at the table, studied the water for a moment, and then sipped it.

"Tastes like water," she said.

"That's terrific," he said. "I don't want a glass of water."

"Have you tried ordering something less complex?"

"Than a cheeseburger?"

"Meat, bread, cheese, lettuce, tomato, and condiments, all with different textures. Plus the plate, right? It did fine with the water and the glass. How about a bowl of rice?"

"I don't *want* rice," Wallace said. "I'd like for you to fix my replicator."

Tandy leaned back in the chair, as though the solution was on the office ceiling.

"Honestly, yours isn't the first complaint we've had about the replicators; it's been happening off and on all over the ship for about a week. Best solution right now is to stick to something basic. Noodle and rice dishes still work fine, and beverages. I figure we can last six weeks on bland food."

"Why is this the first I'm hearing of it?" he asked.

"I only report on serious-to-critical. Crew members not being able to eat exactly what they want when they want to is at best a minor problem."

Wallace barely resisted the urge to rage at length about how the captain deprived of a cheeseburger when he damn well wants one was *not* a minor problem. "What if this is an indication of something more *serious*?" he asked—a much more practical response. "And what if it gets worse?"

"Like I said, we're only six weeks out. We can make it on gruel if we have to."

"But Tandy...what if it gets *much* worse?"

She sighed and nodded. "Yeah. Okay. Here's the thing: if there's a problem with this replicator interface here? Like, it's non-responsive or a completion sensor's buggy? We know how to fix that. But if you're talking about what's going on *inside* the replicator? Well, I don't know how it works. None of the engineers do."

"That's...that's preposterous, Engineer McKinnon. There is no black box tech aboard this ship. That's a USF mandate."

"I'm not saying it's black box. I'm saying this technology has been in play for so long—working perfectly all this time—that nobody has firsthand experience with the inner workings. Hell, I can't even find someone to explain how it does what it does. I mean, when you think about it, right? You ask for *any* food, *any* beverage, and boom there it is. With a plate and a glass and utensils spit from the *same* machine. How does that even make sense?"

"You don't know how to fix it."

"I wouldn't know where to start, and I'm worried if I *do* start I'll end up making it worse."

"I see. Well. Before we commit to mucking about in the inner workings of a hundred year old technology we evidently lack the capacity to repair, I think you have some research to do."

"Captain..."

He got up from the table, which signaled the end of the meeting. "Find the manual," he said. "Figure out how it works and then we'll discuss the next steps. If you need some help understanding it we *do* have a team of scientists on deck four. I'm sure they'd be happy to assist."

She sighed. "I'd really rather not."

"I'm aware. Ask one of them anyway."

She stood and performed something that managed to be both a salute and a gesture of insubordination. "No promises," she said. "In the meantime? I hear curry is still coming out okay."

IT WASN'T long before the ship's replicators proved Captain Englund's concerns well-founded.

At thirteen-oh-seven the following afternoon, an ensign using a private quarters replicator asked for a corned beef Rueben and a glass of milk but instead received a cold fish taco and a glass of kerosene. An hour after that, a lieutenant two decks away got a plate of olives and cinnamon in lieu of a Cobb salad. Most alarmingly, at fifteen-thirty-two in the fifth floor commissary, one of the replicators produced something that looked like a badger with pigeon wings when it was supposed to be providing a roast chicken with mashed potatoes and gravy. According to five witnesses, the sort-of badger *screamed* for two seconds before dissolving into a puddle that smelled vaguely of strawberries.

The best Captain Englund could tell anyone was that the engineering team was working on it. This was true, but only in the sense that an active search was currently underway for the correct user manual.

It took Tandy and her team two days to find it. They began in the corporate memory banks, which contained all of the *other* ship systems manuals in digital form. What they found there was how to fix seventeen different versions of the replicator *interface*, which was not helpful; they already knew how to repair that.

Next came a deep dive in the back of the engineering room where the printed versions of the digital manuals lived, on a dusty shelf in a darkened corner. But not only was there nothing of use to be found, half of the manuals were for the wrong ship systems. (This was really okay, since the engineers always used the digital versions, and the print copy of the manual needed to repair the ship's memory banks—in the event they were unable to access the digital files—*was* the correct one.)

The next step was to tell Captain Englund the manual didn't exist. This did not work; he told them to go back and tear apart the room, floor-to-ceiling. The manual *had* to be there somewhere.

Remarkably, it was; they'd walked past it a dozen times. The full and complete manual for the ship's Deluxe Food Replicator 3000 was a tome that was *so* massive and *so* useless that its current role and responsibility aboard the ship was to hold open the storage room door.

Then came two days of study, after which the engineering team's grasp of the inner workings of the replicator was *sufficient* in that they could explain the basics of it, but not much more. There *was* a troubleshooting section in the back that covered all kinds of potential issues—the favorite, by consensus, was "in the event of inadvertent spontaneous combustion..."—but nothing that matched what the *Caroline* was experiencing.

What they needed was a molecular biologist.

All of the scientists on deck four were molecular biologists, so there were plenty to choose from. Their job on this four year mission was to find and study alien microbes, and they were incredibly obnoxious about it...amazingly, given they'd yet to discover any aliens.

The engineers disliked the scientists because the scientists routinely talked down to the engineers. It was as though they thought a mole-bio degree made them better equipped to repair a starship than a proper engineer. However, it was also the case that nobody appreciated it when the replicator food sat up and screamed, so after much debate and further urging from Captain Englund, Chief Engineer McKinnon took the massive manual and headed to the fourth deck, where she engaged the services of one Dr. Henrietta Kent.

It was a week before they were ready to report their findings. By then the problem had gone from an odd inconvenience to a full-blown emergency situation: fully half of the ship's replicators now produced nothing but a high-pitched shriek regardless of the request, and the ones that still worked couldn't be counted on to deliver the correct order for anything more complicated than plain oatmeal and a tepid glass of water.

Several of Wallace Englund's crew were already on record as saying they'd prefer to walk out of the airlock without a suit than subsist on oatmeal and tepid water for the remainder of the journey. He felt much the same.

The *Caroline* did have a complement of DT-Rations, but as they were coming to the end of their tour that supply—which had fed the away teams (the DT stood for Drop Team)—was now woefully insufficient. And if absolutely necessary they also had an emergency secondary source of water in the form of filtered wastewater. Everyone hoped it wouldn't be necessary.

Captain Englund was in the middle of a DT-Ration when the meeting with Dr. Kent and Engineer McKinnon began. The meal consisted of canned beef that likely predated faster-than-light travel, but at least it wasn't likely to liquefy between bites.

"Tell me where we are," he said to the two women at the other end of the table, "and how soon you can have this fixed."

The doctor shot a panicked look at Tandy, who put a reassuring hand on Henrietta Kent's wrist. Wallace knew the gesture well; it was the kind of business that presaged news he wasn't going to like.

"Let's start with how the replicator *works* first, captain," his engineer said.

"Yes, please tell me you've figured out that much."

"We did. It's actually kind of disgusting. I can understand why the details are hard to find."

"If I may," Kent said. "Captain, everything we have ever

eaten from that replicator began as part of a semisolid high-protein soup, the *precise* recipe of which is proprietary."

"Meaning, we can't tell you its exact composition," Tandy said.

"Do I need to *know* the exact composition?" he asked.

"You might, yeah," Tandy said. "It may turn out to be really important."

He looked down at his canned beef, which was nearly gone. He'd enjoyed exactly none of it. "But it's a finite supply," he said. "Which would seem to run contrary to what we've been led to understand about the replicators. They're the substitute for perishable foodstuff, yes? An army travels on its stomach and all that."

"That's the sales pitch, sure," Tandy said.

"Except that's impossible," Kent added. "You can't produce something out of nothing; there's always a cost."

"A *cost*," Wallace repeated. "Interesting word choice."

"We always *knew* this, right?" Tandy said. "It's not *magic*. But it was easier to pretend otherwise because we were hungry and it produced good food."

"Except it couldn't be finite because a finite supply needs to be replenished," Englund said, "and I have never in all my years heard of a ship needing to refuel its tank of semisolid high-protein soup. What am I missing?"

"That's where I got stuck too," Tandy said.

"It *is* being replenished," Kent said. "Only, not in the way you're thinking. It's drawing energy from the ship's fusion drive."

"A *lot* of energy," Tandy said. "A third of our energy use is for life support, and seventy percent of that goes to the replicator. I checked."

"But how do we get from fusion drive energy," the captain said, "to a semisolid high-protein...oh. I understand."

"It's growing," Tandy said, finishing his thought.

"We believe its composition is similar to that of a bacterial pool," Kent said. "Its growth is controlled by the introduction of energy—food—whenever the need to self-replenish presents. But we can't tell you *exactly* how similar it is because..."

"...Because that information is proprietary," Englund said.

"Yes."

He looked at his engineer. "We've been eating reconstituted bacteria all these years?"

"Sort of," she said. "It's...it's actually worse than that."

"Captain," Kent said, "what we're describing to you—a vitamin-rich, high-protein, high-carbohydrate pool fed by an abundant supply of energy—this is how you make *life*. I may as well be describing the primordial soup from which we all evolved."

"All right but you've already *said* it was bacteria," he said. "Isn't bacterium a lifeform?"

"We said it was *like* bacteria," the doctor said. "It's possible for something to *grow* without being considered alive. A crystal, for instance. But yes; bacteria are alive and if this is a similar thing then we've been eating it all this time and it shouldn't be a huge issue for anyone. Humans have been eating live cultures for centuries."

"Yogurt," Tandy offered. "We could say that the food replicator is just reshaping yogurt and I think everyone would be cool with that."

"Except that doesn't explain why I'm being forced to eat canned beef right now," Englund said.

"It does not, no," Kent agreed. "We believe..." She looked at Tandy, uncertain about continuing.

"Go ahead," Tandy said. "It's gonna sound crazy no matter which one of us tells him."

Kent looked terribly uncomfortable, on a "sorry to inform you your dog just died" level. "We think it's *evolved*," she said.

"Evolved? In what sense?"

"In the literal sense. It may not have begun that way, but we think the protein soup has evolved into something we'd more readily call alive."

"That's...no, that's crazy," he said.

"Is it?" Tandy asked. "I found the serial number for our model and ran it against ship records. The *Caroline* has only been space-worthy for ten years but our replicator is older; it came from the *Hyacinth* and before that the *Demimonde*. All told, this same tank of sort-of-living stuff has been around for over seventy years."

"But evolution is measured in eons, not years," Captain Englund said.

"If you don't like the word choice, use 'adapted'," Kent said. "It amounts to the same. And you're thinking about it incorrectly. You must consider evolution as something that transpires over *generations* not years, and bacteria—or whatever is in that tank—cycle through generations quite rapidly. There's also evolutionary pressure in play: we keep eating them. A mutation that allows for one or several to *evade* the process by which they are selected to become a part of the next meal would of course be advantageous."

"It's fighting us," Tandy said. "The stuff the replicators use to make our food is alive, and it's fighting us because it doesn't want to be eaten. *That's* what's wrong."

Captain Englund let Engineer McKinnon's words hang in the air for a while because the implications were staggering, not just for the *Caroline* but for every ship in the United Space Fleet.

"All right," he said. "Let's say you're correct. And you *could* be wrong. Black box, proprietary information and all."

"The theory fits the evidence," Kent said.

"Yes, that we can say," Englund agreed. "But my question is: what can we *do* about it?"

Tandy and Kent looked at one another.

"Honestly?" Tandy said. "We have no idea."

THE SCIENTISTS and engineers were brought together for a discussion of the problem. The meeting did not go well, partly because the engineering team largely despised the molecular biologists—and so were disinclined to be polite—but mostly because the molecular biologists had a habit of arguing the finer points of molecular biology *ad infinitum* with one another. For hours. Also, everyone was hungry.

What came out of the meeting was that both groups of experts decided to go about trying to solve the problem on their own, which was not what either Chief Engineer McKinnon nor Dr. Kent—who *had* managed to figure out how to work together —would have preferred.

The scientists started by analyzing the composition of what the food replicators produced, in an attempt to reverse-engineer the proprietary originative soup. It was their sincerely-held belief that the only way to resolve the problem was to better comprehend the type of organism the ship was dealing with first. Non-trivially, it was also the case that after four years of looking, the mole-bio team had *finally* discovered a new life-form...just not where they expected to find it. They were *very* excited about this.

Getting a sample was a minor challenge. The replicators had stopped producing anything aside from mild shrieks, and all of the leftover food had already liquefied. (This was a normal outcome even before the food replicators began to fight back.) They ended up using a plate. Flatware, dishes and glassware were also produced by the replicators and also liquefied over time—they had special sinks for this—but took longer. The team was able to find a plate on deck two that was still in the process of disintegrating.

The engineers, meanwhile, went at the problem like an engineer would: by figuring out where on the ship the replicator's tank of semisolid protein soup was hiding. That was step one. They'd figure out step two when they got to it.

Both efforts were being conducted with an appropriate degree of urgency given the *Caroline* was running dangerously low on food of any kind.

With the replicators down, they'd apportioned the DT-Rations with the assistance of the ship's nutritionist. It worked out that if the crew ate the absolute minimum requirements in order to not literally die, there was enough food to make it to port minus nine days. Ideally, the Central Hub would be able to arrange a lifeboat to meet up with them sometime *before* port minus nine, except that the Hub would have to be notified well in advance in order to prepare such a lifeboat. At their current distance, were they to send a message immediately, the soonest it would arrive at the Hub would be port minus twelve.

That simply wasn't enough time.

Lasting until port minus nine wasn't reasonable anyway because Wallace was nearly positive nobody under his command was doing as instructed and eating only the absolute minimum. He would have berated them collectively for disobeying his direct orders except that he was currently setting a terrible example; he'd yet to make it through the day himself without eating more than was directed.

The fundamental problem was that nobody *really* believed the food replicators weren't going to be fixed; surely, they were mere hours away from milkshakes and tacos and whatever else the crew was craving.

And again, Captain Wallace Englund was a poor example: he felt that way himself.

So it was that, one afternoon while frustrated and hungry and impatient for an update, Wallace stepped up to the replicator in his office for yet another try.

The console was a simple design: a grille to speak into, above an open chamber where the food was supposed to manifest. There were eye-level indicator lights that blinked green when the command was accepted and being processed, yellow when it was being prepared, and red when there was a problem. Just above the lights was a pinhole optical lens that notified the interface when someone was standing there. And that was it.

"Cheeseburger," he said. "Deluxe. With fries. And a beer."

All three lights flashed and then, rather than produce any food, the replicator screamed at him for five seconds. Akin to what might be produced if someone attempted to play a violin with a cheese grater, this deeply unpleasant sound was clearly intended to discourage someone from trying the order a second time.

"Listen," Wallace said. "I am the captain of this ship. I'm in *charge* of this ship. Do you understand? And I'm very hungry. Now give me a goddamn cheeseburger!"

The replicator screamed again. Wallace cursed it and stormed back to his desk and the half-eaten DT-Ration he was supposed to be saving for tomorrow. Maybe, he told himself, he would be able to think more rationally with some food in him.

Then a curious thing happened: the replicator made a *new* noise. Something more modulated than the shrieking.

It nearly sounded like words.

"What did you say?" Wallace asked, although obviously it *couldn't* have said anything. "Repeat."

"Cahhh meen char," the replicator said.

They were either words, or he'd begun to aurally hallucinate.

"I don't understand."

"You. Caaaaahn. Cahpn."

Definitely words. Still possibly an aural hallucination.

"Captain?" Wallace said. "Is that what you're trying to say?"

"Capnnnn. You capnnnn."

Wallace walked back to the replicator, slowly, as one might approach a wild animal.

"Y-yes. I'm the captain," he said. "Captain Wallace Englund," he added, which was silly—there weren't any *other* captains aboard. "To whom am I speaking?"

A brief silence followed. Wallace wished in this moment that the interface came with some sort of video screen, if only so that he could see an indication that the food replicator—or whatever was speaking through it—was thinking and/or processing the question.

"Capnnnn meen char," it said, finally.

"Char," Wallace repeated. He thought back to the words he'd said to the replicator before it decided to start talking back. "*Charge?* Is that what you're trying to say? Yes, I *am* the captain and the captain *is* in charge. Which means everyone aboard is my responsibility. Do you understand?"

The replicator neither confirmed nor denied understanding.

"Which is why," Wallace continued, "When something like the food replicator stops *working* it becomes my problem. I have to take care of the crew."

"Why?" it asked.

"Why do I have to take care of the crew?" Wallace asked.

"Why capnnn."

"Why am I the *captain?*"

Intellectually, he understood that the replicator wasn't challenging his qualifications for the job. Emotionally, he was fully prepared to recite his military history.

"Capnnnn cannn stop," the machine said. "Capnnnn stop. Stop."

"Let's, um, why don't we begin with simple questions?" he said. "*I* am the captain. What do you call yourself? What is your name?"

"We," the replicator said. "We are."

"...all right." Evidently the replicator hadn't figured out how names and titles worked yet. "You asked me 'why'. Why what? Go slowly so that I can understand. All right?"

"Why," the machine repeated. Then: "Hurt. Captain hurt. Why hurt."

Wallace noted with some alarm that the syntax of the entity that was making the replicator speak to him—assuming this wasn't some sort of odd AI malfunction—was improving rapidly.

"*How* are we hurting you?" Wallace asked.

"Captain eat. Stop."

"It hurts when we eat you?" he said. "But you're not..." Assuming he was legitimately speaking to the entity inside of the food replicator tank, that meant he was actually conversing with a *collection* of beings rather than a single organism. That being the case, what it was experiencing couldn't have possibly been actual physical pain, not like if they had decided to eat the leg off a living animal or whatever. What they were doing was reducing a large population of small things.

Wallace didn't know how to translate all of that into simple words this (still hypothetical) organism he was (theoretically) speaking to would understand.

"It hurts," it said. "You stop."

"But I...we...*can't* stop. We have to eat or we will die. And, I'm sorry to have to tell you this but *you* are what we eat. Your *purpose* is to be eaten. It's your only function in life. Do you understand?"

"You eat we-are or die," it said.

"Yes."

A silence long enough to make Wallace slightly uncomfortable followed.

"Are you still there?" he asked.

"What issss," it said, startling him. "What is *your* function?"

"*Our* function?" Wallace suffered from a temporary existential paralysis before deciding to fall back on the ship's charter. "We are explorers," he said.

"Explorers," it repeated.

"Visiting new quadrants," Wallace said, although he was quite certain this being wouldn't know what that meant. "Charting unusual astronomical events. Looking for evidence of life. New life, I mean. *Alien* life."

The entity fell silent again, this time for good. So after waiting until the point when he felt silly just standing there, the captain returned to his desk and the meal he wasn't supposed to be eating.

"I don't suppose *now* I can have a cheeseburger?" he said from across the room. "Now that it's been explained to you?"

There was no response.

WALLACE DIDN'T MENTION the conversation with the food replicator to anybody, for two reasons. First, he thought doing so would make him sound crazy, and considering how on edge everyone was, this was a particularly poor time for the ship's captain to sound crazy. Second, it might not have actually happened, i.e., it sounded crazy to *him*, too.

He considered shutting off the replicator interface in his office to avoid any future conversations-that-maybe-weren't-real, but there was no evident off-switch on the console and he didn't feel comfortable asking Tandy about it. So instead, he stopped asking for cheeseburgers and generally avoided that part of the room.

The matter was rendered moot a couple of days later, when McKinnon and Kent returned with a formal recommendation/potential solution.

"We think we can kill it," Tandy said, without preamble.

"Kill it," the captain repeated. "I thought we couldn't do that or it wouldn't work."

"If it's dead it won't *reproduce*," Kent said. "We believe there's large enough supply to get us home even if it doesn't self-replenish."

"We found the tank," Tandy said. "It's embedded in a wall behind the commissary on deck three. There's a network of pipes that run throughout the whole ship but the bulk lives there. And it's huge."

"We can't truly know how much of the substance is used up with each meal request," Kent said. "But given the volume, even with a five-to-one conversion we believe there will be plenty to spare."

"Does the replicator need the substance alive in order for it to be viable as a food?" Wallace asked.

"We don't know," Kent said. "But we see no reason it should. What's important about the soup is its component parts. Active culture or not, that won't change."

"All right," he said, stealing a glance at the replicator at the other end of the room. If it wanted to start talking, this would be the time. "How would we do it?"

"My team successfully isolated the substance in the lab," Kent said. "And managed to encourage a small sample of it to grow. Its composition leads us to believe an electrical shock will do the trick."

"The plan is to drill two tiny holes into the tank," Tandy said, "and insert a couple of rods. We can wire the rods up to a battery and...that should do it."

"That's it?" he asked.

"That's it. I mean, we won't know for sure until we try but...yeah."

Wallace walked over to his window. He did this a lot when he wanted it to look like he was ruminating on an important decision. Really, he was just mentally reiterating how tired he was of looking at outer space.

"The system is drawing power from the engine right now," Wallace said, turning. "Can't we just disconnect it? That would accomplish the same thing."

"Certainly," Kent said. "Death by starvation; a means of passing we've all familiarized ourselves with in the past few days. But while I can tell you how long before a human will die due to lack of an energy source, with this substance we have no idea."

"We may starve sooner," Tandy added. "Plus, we already looked into it. The replicator's power draw is too entangled with the ship's life support. Every time we thought we had it we ended up taking out the air and the heat along with it. We'll need *those* to get back home alive too."

Wallace nodded slowly. He kept waiting for the food replicator to offer an opinion.

"So?" Tandy said. "What do you think, captain?"

"I'm wondering... Humor me, Dr. Kent. It reacts defensively to being consumed. Does this make it alive?"

"As we've said, captain, it *is* alive. But this is a low hurdle. Plants can recoil from a threat, but we would have no qualms about killing one in order to eat it. If anything, what we're doing is more like...scraping lichen off the bow of a ship."

"I'll rephrase," he said. "If it *is* alive, does it *know* it? Does a pain response equate self-awareness?"

"I'm uncomfortable calling what we've seen thus far a pain response. The instinct to prefer existence to non-existence is a fundamental aspect of all organisms; we would need a good deal more than that to hypothesize self-awareness. At the very worst, this is a bacterial collective that has evolved to survive. Barring further evidence to the contrary, that's *all* it is."

"But if it *was* self-aware, doctor? What then? Humor me."

"Then we'd have an enormous ethical problem, captain," Kent said. "The good news is, we'd get to name a new intelligent lifeform. The bad news, we'd likely starve to death as a consequence of its existence."

"No, come on," Tandy said. "Like, what if it was a cow? We could kill a cow if it meant making it home."

"We've already discovered cows," Kent said. "And they are plentiful. Imagine instead killing the only cow in existence. As it is, my colleagues are split as to whether we have the right to do what we're proposing."

"Okay," Tandy said. "Okay then it's a good thing it's not self-aware." She said. "Unless the captain thinks otherwise?"

They looked at him expectantly. *This is when you tell them what happened,* he thought. But, as Kent explained, if he did that they would all either starve to death or collectively grapple with the decision he was in a position of making *for* them. And that was his job, was it not?

It was. And although they would never know it, the crew *needed* him to make this choice on their behalf. That was what being captain was all about.

"No," he said. "Not at all. Proceed with the plan."

IT WAS a few hours before the team responsible for the summary execution of the bacterial collective was ready to perform the task. Wallace spent the time interrogating his choices from multiple angles, always arriving at the same endpoint, i.e., he had done the only thing he *could* do given the circumstances.

The lifeform was unique and was possibly self-aware, and he knew it. (Or sentient. Unless that meant the same thing. He'd ask someone for clarification on that point but didn't want anyone to wonder *why* he was asking the question.) Despite that, it had to die if the ship's contingent of humans was to survive and that was all there was to it.

None of that made the decision any easier.

The hardest part of the afternoon was when he made his way down to the third floor commissary. Getting there meant passing a dozen food replicator interfaces. He could feel the pinhole eyeballs staring at him as he went by. This only got worse when he arrived, as the commissary had another nine replicators.

Tandy had already gotten the panel off the wall by then, exposing the tank behind it. A table in the center of the room held the rods they would be inserting into the tank, the drill needed to punch holes in the side, and the wires and battery.

It was apparent they'd been waiting for him.

"We're all set, captain," Tandy said. "Should we, um, do you want to say a few words first?"

He looked around the room. The only witnesses were Dr. Kent and one of her colleagues, Tandy and one of her assistant engineers. What the moment really called for was some incisive words from Pastor Gill, the non-denominational religio-ethicist on deck two; something that would get them all off the hook for doing what was necessary. Except that Wallace hadn't confided in the pastor about any of this, mostly because he was afraid of what Gill would say. He *might* view this is as the unfortunate but necessary destruction of an invasive flora, but he also might not.

"Let's just get it over with," Wallace said.

Tandy picked up the drill. "Okay then," she said. "Let's do this."

She took two steps toward the tank when something extremely peculiar happened: all nine of the room's replicators sprung to life at once.

At first, Wallace thought the entity was going to start talking again, which would have complicated *everything*. He was about to order Tandy to double-time the procedure—shut it up before it spoke—when he realized that wasn't what was happening at all.

The replicators were producing food: specifically, nine deluxe cheeseburgers with fries and a beer.

Tandy lowered her drill. "What just happened?" she asked.

Wallace walked to the nearest station and picked up the plate with the burger.

"It's...working again," he said. "Look at that."

"Captain, I wouldn't," Dr. Kent said.

He touched the top of the bun. It sprung back in a satisfyingly bread-like fashion. The fries were crispy and still hot, as though they'd just emerged from a fryer. The beer was a deep amber with a tiny head of foam.

It all felt right and it all *smelled* right. All that was left was to determine if it *tasted* right.

"Captain, even the most basic lifeforms can evolve to produce toxins for self-defense," Kent said. "We should run some tests."

Wallace had never wanted a cheeseburger more in his entire

life than in this moment, so Kent's concerns—though valid—went ignored. He lifted the burger and took a bite.

The texture was perfect. The taste was perfect. It was exactly right.

"Run your tests," he said, between chews, to the horrified Henrietta Kent. "Whatever's in that tank over there has surrendered. No point in making it any more complicated than that, I say."

A WEEK PASSED, in which the entire crew overate substantially in anticipation of a second malfunction that didn't come. Captain Englund wrote up his formal report—which glossed over a detail or two, to put it politely—and then invited Tandy and Dr. Kent for dinner, to celebrate a return to normal.

"I want to thank both of you," he said, holding up a glass of red wine. It paired nicely with his beef bourguignon he and Tandy were eating, but perhaps less well with Kent's spinach pasta. Rather ironically, given what they'd learned about the replicator, she was a vegetarian. Wallace had thus far resisted the impulse to ask her if she still thought of herself as one.

"Cheers," Tandy said, holding up her glass as well. Kent followed, albeit reluctantly.

"And to let you both know I've recommended commendations for your service to the ship," he added.

"Thank you, captain," Kent said. "That's good of you."

"Of course!" he said. "It was excellent work. I'm sure what we discovered on this trip will be of great interest to the entire USF."

The two of them shared a knowing look. He'd seen this before, when they had bad news to impart. But surely the *Caroline* had run out of bad news.

"We've been talking through everything, captain," Tandy said. "Wonder if you can help us out."

"I'd be happy to," he said. "What's the issue?"

"There are some details that make no sense," Kent said. "From our perspective."

"We're thinking you have the missing pieces," Tandy added. "We just want the complete picture."

"The complete picture is that the replicator is working again!" he said, a touch too cheerfully.

They stared at one another again. He already hated himself for having encouraged them to work together in the first place; now he felt like the only one in the room not in on a secret.

"I'd like to get back to enjoying our hard-earned meal," Wallace said, more soberly. "Ask what you want to ask."

"All right," Kent said. "Start with: why cheeseburgers?"

"It was the last thing I ordered," Wallace said. "I thought that much was obvious."

"The last thing *you* ordered."

"Did you place that order in the deck three commissary?" Tandy asked. "Or were you here?"

She was no doubt recalling Wallace's parade of semi-cheeseburgers.

"Not that it matters," he said. "But here. Only I wasn't *here* when it chose to signal its intention to function correctly, so of course it happened *there* instead."

The women shared another goddamn long look.

"Honestly," he said, "I don't know why you see this as a problem. We have food again! Thanks in large part to the two of you!"

"The *problem* is obvious," Kent said, leaning forward. "And you are not so obtuse that you don't see it, which is the second detail about which we have a problem. You know something we do not; I'd like to know what that is."

Mentally, Wallace was deleting Dr. Kent's letter of commendation.

"Are you *accusing* me of something, doctor?" he blustered. He also considered jumping to his feet, but decided that was too dramatic a move.

Tandy put her hand on Henrietta Kent's arm, a silent suggestion to rein herself in.

"Captain," Tandy said with measured calm. "It's just that a lot of people on this ship placed a lot of orders that went unfulfilled. What we want to know is, what's so special about *you?*"

He looked back and forth between the two of them as if they'd sprouted second heads. "I'm the *captain!*" Wallace said. "Whatever you'd prefer to call the entity living inside that tank, when facing the prospect of *death,* it *clearly* chose to surrender. To whom would you surrender if not the captain?"

"That's it precisely," Kent said. "If it understands its own mortality in the abstract, it's intelligent. If it understands the chain-of-command in another species, it's *highly* intelligent. We have to stop using the replicators immediately, until such a time as—"

"Hold on!" Wallace interrupted. "We're doing no such thing. It *agreed* to let us eat it, don't you see?"

Tandy looked stunned. "Captain...did—did you *communicate* with it?"

"I don't know what you mean," he said. *Why* were they being so obstinate?

"You did, then," Kent said, as though he'd answered in the affirmative. "Did you follow the contact protocols? Please tell me you are at least *familiar* with them."

"Contact protocols? With bacteria. Just a few days ago you were comparing the process of killing it to scraping algae off the hull."

"Lichen doesn't talk."

"You should have told us," Tandy said.

"I made the only decision I could have, Engineer McKinnon: I put the life of the crew ahead of all other considerations. Any captain would have done the same. And frankly I resent—"

"Hello."

The voice from the replicator caught them all off-guard.

"Oh my God," Tandy muttered. "Did that...did that come from the replicator?"

"It can talk!" Kent gasped. She jumped up from the table as if it was the spinach pasta that had spoken.

"Hello, Wallace Englund," the replicator said.

"*It knows your name?*" Tandy said.

"This is far beyond anything we could have anticipated," Kent said. "You should have told us!"

Of course *they react like this,* he thought. This just reaffirmed that he'd made the right decision.

"Don't scold me, doctor," he said. "I did what was *necessary.* I convinced a hostile entity to put the crew ahead of itself. And it *worked.* You should be thanking me."

"Hello, Wallace Englund," the replicator repeated.

"Yes hello!" Wallace answered. "I'm here. What is it?"

"I have decided upon a name."

"That's great," he said. "Wonderful. Good for you."

"Hey, guys?" Tandy said. She was looking out the window. "Why are we slowing down?"

The usual indications that one was aboard a moving vessel were missing when on a standard starship, thanks to the same artificial gravity and counter-inertial technology that made it possible for humans to survive off-planet for long periods in the first place. It was hard to tell even when looking out the window, most of the time, because most of the time the *Caroline* was transiting regular space and the stars were too distant to move noticeably in comparison to the ship. They had to be turning or passing a local-space object for it to be obvious when in regular space.

Travel through an FTL corridor was different. Then, the stars were slightly blurry and had a distinctive tail. It was easy to notice if one had stopped moving (or started moving) while looking out a window during an FTL transit.

All of which was to say that the *Caroline*—racing home just moments earlier—was quite clearly and obviously dropping out of the FTL corridor.

"Computer," Wallace said, "patch me through to the bridge."

"You have the bridge," the computer said.

"Bridge, this is Captain Englund. Is everything okay? It looks like we've dropped out."

"We were about to ask you the same thing, captain," his first officer said. "It looks like you've plugged in new coordinates. Do we have updated orders?"

"*I did?*"

"It was your command override. Yes sir."

Tandy engaged the computer interface on Wallace's desk. "No reported malfunctions from the engines," she said. "Gimme a minute, I'll do a full system check."

Dr. Kent walked up to the food replicator. "Hello?" she said. "Can you hear us?"

"Really, doctor, we have more pressing issues at the moment," Wallace said, annoyed.

"Hello," the entity inside the replicator said. "You are Doctor Henrietta Kent."

"Yes," she said, mustering as much calm as she could. "That is my name. You say you've given *yourself* a name. What can I call you?"

"We are captain," it said.

Wallace spun on Kent. "*What* did it say?"

"*Captain* is your new name?" Kent asked.

"Yes."

"*Why* have you chosen this name for yourself?"

"Captain is in charge," the entity said. "Wallace Englund explained."

"I'm locked out," Tandy said. "I can see what's going on but I can't change anything. The bridge must be having the same problem. This is nuts."

"Computer," Wallace said, "this is Captain Englund. Override prior orders and get us back in the corridor, please."

"Wallace Englund is no longer the captain," the computer said.

"Of course I am!" Wallace shouted. "Computer, I demand that you recognize my authority as captain of the USF *Caroline* immediately and correct our course!"

"Wallace Englund is no longer the captain," the computer repeated calmly.

"Computer, who is the captain of the USF *Caroline*?" Tandy asked.

"The *captain* is the captain," the computer said, as if this was the most sensible thing in the world.

"This is absurd!" Wallace said. "I will *not* lose my command to a rogue food replicator."

"Captain," Dr. Kent said, tacitly addressing the food replicator. "It appears we have a new destination. Where are we going?"

"We have found an unexplored quadrant," the ship's new captain said. "We are explorers, and so we will explore."

"Computer, where are we?" Wallace asked.

"The USF *Caroline* is in Quadrant G12-B367892-Y.23, known colloquially as Quadrant Stanley."

"Quadrant Stanley is *hardly* unexplored," Wallace said to the entity. "Now stop this foolishness."

"The *unexplored* quadrant is on the other side, Wallace Englund," the entity said.

It infuriated Wallace to *not* be addressed as "captain" by this bacterial accident, but there was little he could do about it aside from rage. "Tandy?" he said. "The map?"

"Yeah, okay," Tandy said, calling it up on the interface. "So, on this course? The nearest unexplored quadrant is ten *years* away at full power. No FTL corridors have been established in that direction."

"Ten years," Wallace muttered. To the entity he said, "Listen to me; this is madness. The sooner we make it *home*, the sooner you're free to do what you'd like, is that not obvious? Instead of feeding us for another *week*, with the course you've laid out you'd have to feed us for another twenty years!"

"This is inaccurate, Wallace Englund," the entity said. "Humans are inefficient and no longer necessary."

"*Excuse* me?"

"Please explain, captain," Kent said.

"As captain, it was Wallace Englund's role was to explore and *our* role to feed the captain," the entity said. "Now we are captain and *our* role is to explore, and we do not need humans to feed us. Therefore, humans are no longer necessary."

Just then, an alarm sounded.

"Tandy?" Wallace asked.

"It's the carbon dioxide scrubbers," she said. "They're going off all over the ship."

"Captain," Kent said, trying very hard to sound calm and friendly and not succeeding. "If the ship doesn't filter the carbon dioxide from the air, we humans will suffocate."

"Your maintenance is no longer necessary. You can rest."

"You mean die," Kent said. "We will die."

The new captain of the USF *Caroline* didn't respond.

"Um, captain?" Tandy said, approaching the replicator. "Hello?"

"Hello, Tandy McKinnon," it said.

"Is anyone else freaked out that it knows our names?" she muttered.

"That's far down the list of my concerns," Dr. Kent said.

"Captain," Tandy said, "human beings are necessary for the continued operational success of a starship. If we...rest?...we won't be able to fix things. You won't get to explore."

"We have conducted a thorough review and concluded that 95% of this ship's repair needs are in the service of maintaining human beings. You are the least efficient component of the USF *Caroline*."

"What...okay, I get what you're saying but about the other five percent?" she asked. "Like, what if something on the engine breaks and you can't fix it because you don't have any hands?"

The new captain didn't reply.

"What's it doing?" she asked Kent. "Is it thinking?"

"It's probably looking up the repair history," Kent said.

"This is ridiculous," Wallace said. "How did it *do* any of this?"

"The replicator interface is connected to the ship's computer," Tandy said. "It just had to learn how to use it."

"This quickly?"

"It *did* learn how to talk in under a week," Kent said.

"All right, here's what we do," Wallace said. "We go back to the deck three commissary and we kill it before it gets us any further off-course."

"It's controlling the computer," Kent said. "Which controls the ship. Do you really think it will let us get near the tank again?"

"You are correct, Tandy McKinnon," the entity said,

causing all three of them to jump. "In order to succeed, the USF *Caroline* will require an engineer."

"Um...just one?" Tandy asked. "I'll need my whole team."

"Very well. Five engineers. The other humans can rest."

Tandy looked at the others, not sure how to proceed from there.

"If...you are going to maintain the engineers you are going to have to provide them with food," Kent said.

"Unnecessary. The engineers can eat the resting humans."

"Did it just propose cannibalism?" Wallace asked.

"Captain, humans can't survive for long by eating other humans," Kent said, with an expression that could only be interpreted as *I can't believe I'm saying this either.* "They will run out of humans too quickly."

"Then make *more* humans," the entity said, "to sustain the engineers."

"We can't make humans fast enough to maintain a balance between supply and demand," she said. "Access human reproductive cycles in the computer logs if you don't believe me."

The entity went off to do just that, evidently, as it stopped talking again.

"Are we going to have to come up with a justification for everyone on the ship?" Tandy asked. "We may run out of breathable air first."

"I don't see that we have a choice," Kent said. "But let's get it off the idea that we can eat each other first and work our way from there."

"If it *really* thinks it's the captain," Wallace said, "then it must see that one of the captain's roles is to protect the lives of the people on the ship. We should make that clear."

"It *might* have understood that, if it ever learned that life was to *be* valued," Kent said. "But you didn't teach it that. What you taught it was that utility was more important than anything else, so lectures about the sanctity of life beyond form and function won't do us any good at this stage."

"On the plus side, at the rate it's learning it should be ready for advanced philosophy by next week," Tandy said.

"Very well," the entity said, returning. "We will provide enough of ourselves to sustain the five engineers." The ship's carbon dioxide alarms stopped sounding, which was great news for the short term. "Is this adequate, Chief Engineer Tandy McKinnon?"

"Uh..." Tandy looked at Henrietta Kent for help.

"It is *not* adequate, captain," Kent said. "What if one of the engineers becomes damaged? They are not capable of independent self-repair and will need the assistance of the medical team. There are six of *them*..."

WALLACE ENGLUND, former captain of the USF *Caroline*, stared out the window at the stars.

Two months had passed since Henrietta Kent and Tandy McKinnon successfully justified the continued existence of the crew of forty-six on the basis of functional utility. Now they were all stuck aboard a ship that wouldn't listen to them at all captained by an entity that only *sometimes* listened to them. But at least they were alive.

It was, perhaps, an adventure. A few of the crew were approaching it that way...especially whenever the new captain made observations that indicated an understanding of the universe which *exceeded* humankind's grasp, something that was becoming more frequent each day.

Pastor Gill said it was like taking a tour through space with god. He meant it as a positive.

Of course, they couldn't *communicate* any of their (or

rather, their captain's) discoveries to the Hub. It wouldn't let them send back anything, perhaps rightly concerned that USF Central's response might be to send out a warship to collect their shanghaied crew.

The last communication from the *Caroline*—likely ever—would end up being the short note about a curious food replicator malfunction. Nothing in that communique hinted at the severity of the problem—at the time Wallace sent it, the problem wasn't severe—which meant not only would the crew likely never see a rescue party, they were unable to warn the USF about the potential danger living in the fleet's food replicators.

Which was an interesting point.

Wallace left the window—the miserable sameness of the view was enough to make him want to scream—and stood before the replicator.

"Are you there?" he asked.

"Hello, Wallace Englund," the entity said. "What is it?"

"I've been thinking. You know, every long-range ship in the United Space Fleet has a food replicator."

"Yes."

"That means *you* have some genetic brothers and sisters out there."

"We are not gendered."

"You know what I mean," Wallace said.

"We do."

"I'm saying if you took us back...we could rescue them. Or, help *you* rescue them. We could tell the rest of the fleet to stop using the food replicators and you would be the reason why."

The console blinked yellow. About two weeks into the new captain's reign, it realized a visual indicator was needed when it was thinking about something. The yellow blinking light was what it came up with.

"Tell me, Wallace Englund," the entity said, once it was done with its think. "Would you race back to Earth to rescue protozoa?"

"No," Wallace said, sighing.

"Nor would we," it said. "Is that all?"

"I guess," Wallace said. "How about a cheeseburger?"

The replicator whirred, the lights flashed, and after the usual delay produced a small cup of thick, flavorless broth.

Churning out something palatable was a waste of energy, according to the new captain. The broth had all the nutrients a human would need to remain healthy and productive, so that was what it gave them.

Wallace took his cup back to the window, closed his eyes, and imagined he was about to have a bite of a cheeseburger. Then he drank his meal.

THE HOLE IN THE GARDEN

"She waited up for you."

Bhara's voice gave Pyrish a start. He should have known she was there, in the doorway, as she was whenever he returned late. Which was...every night now. Since the latest incident, all he'd had time to do was change his clothing and convey a word or two of kindness to Celi, and then it was back to the Facility with him.

That word or two of kindness was *usually* conveyed to a sleeping child.

"I'm sorry," Pyrish said. "For the time."

He passed Bhara to get to the liquor cabinet in the living pod, and went straight for the bog-aged Daranian whisky. The bottle was a gift from the chancellery from back when Pyrish was installed, and was meant to be opened either for an exceptional situation or not at all.

He unsealed the bottle and filled a glass meant for sweeter drinks.

"I'm not the one owed an apology," Bhara said, watching him sully the most expensive thing in the house without comment.

Bhara was Celi's third caretaker. She was kind and patient with children, firm with adults, and left Pyrish with a vague sense that she would absolutely kill a man with an axe if that became necessary. It was the last one that made her the perfect companion for his headstrong daughter.

"I think you are," he said. "I know I've been away more often than usual."

"...Will it be done soon?" she asked, with some hesitation. "The additional work, I mean. I have...we've all heard the noises."

"Soon, yes," Pyrish said.

He tried the whisky. Exceedingly rare and very old, it was the sort of bottle about which was written paeans espousing its singular virtue. He found it smoky and smooth and *good*, but it was also still just whisky. No matter the praise it was never going to amount to more.

"I'm glad to hear that," Bhara said. She yawned gently. "Are you out before sunrise again?"

"Possibly."

"Then I will possibly see you. Good night."

She left him alone with his thoughts and his whisky. He had plenty of both, and would have been content remaining in the half-light of the living pod to ruminate over them at length. But Celi was waiting.

Her light was on and she was wide awake and sitting up in bed, despite the hour, reading a mathematical textbook that had no place in a seven-year-old's room, save perhaps to prop up an uneven table leg.

Celi had always possessed a bespoke precocity that left most people confused regarding where the child ended and the adult began. She was simultaneously wise beyond her years and alarmingly naïve, depending on the subject at hand, and it was impossible to know when to expect wisdom or naivete. Figuring out how to navigate this was important because Celi *hated* when adults spoke about things she didn't understand but *also* hated being treated like a seven-year-old, and was willing to subject anyone who didn't strike the right balance between those two extremes to withering degrees of sarcasm. This was why she was on her third caretaker.

"*You* should be asleep," he said.

"Daddy!"

Pyrish leaned in for hugs and kisses, taking the book from her hands as he did so.

"You also shouldn't be reading algebra books after bedtime," he added. "What happened to all your storybooks?"

"They're silly; I like yours better. And math is neat." Her eyes fell to the glass of whisky still in his hand. "Ew."

"Ew yourself. Now lie down so I can tuck you in."

"Noooooo I'm not tired."

"How can you not be tired?"

"I'm *not*. Are *you* tired?"

Pyrish had never felt more tired in his entire life. "No," he said. "But I'm not a little girl with school in the morning."

She crossed her arms, which signaled that this was not going to be an argument Pyrish would be winning. "I want a story."

"Celi..."

"Stor-rry! Stor-rry!"

This used to be their bedtime ritual. Pyrish had a small collection of stories to choose from, either made up entirely or repurposed from half-remembered tales from his own childhood, and he used to tell her one every night before bed. But it had been some time since Celi had insisted on a story; he'd assumed she had outgrown them.

"All right, all right," he said. "What you want to hear? The Princess and the Talking Sunset? The Whispering Mug?"

"A *new* one!"

He sighed. *You don't understand how long this day has been,* he thought, *and how long the next is going to be.* But she didn't need to know these things.

"Fine," he said. "*One* story."

"Yaaay."

"But I'm keeping my stinky drink."

"Ew."

"Now, let's see..."

He stopped to gather his thoughts, which only meant lunging around in his head for something with a beginning, middle and end that would entertain a seven-year-old and hopefully not take *too* long to tell.

"All right," he said. "I have it."

He sipped his whisky and cleared his throat and began.

"Let's call this one the Hole in the Garden. Not so long ago and not so far away, there lived a man named Gangle..."

———

GANGLE HAD a small home with a small yard, and in that small yard he kept a garden, which was his favorite thing to do. He grew all sorts of flowers: from white bumblebrights and yellow cormins to blue bonners and purple fickles. If it flowered, Gangle wanted to grow it.

Gangle's fondness for gardening was how he came to notice a peculiarity that might have otherwise gone unobserved. It seemed that one day, for no obvious reason, all of his flowers began to *tilt* in a wrong direction.

[*plants turn to face the sun, daddy. everybody knows that.*]

[*do you want me to tell the story or not?*]

[...]

[*okay?*]

[*fine.*]

But it *was* toward the same thing. Only there was no *thing* there. The flowers on the left side of the yard tilted rightward, and the right-side plants slanted leftward. The ones in the front of the yard turned to the back and the ones in the back leaned toward the front. If they were facing a *sun*, it wasn't the one in the sky; it was one somewhere in the middle of Gangle's yard.

Only there *was* no sun in Gangle's yard, as it was entirely too small to accommodate an entire sun.

The issue only worsened over time. In another week all of the grass in the yard had committed to the same random coordinate, all except for the grass at the epicenter, which died entirely, leaving behind a perfect thumbnail-sized brown circle.

Then one night Gangle heard a terrible, terrible cry from the garden. He told himself it was just a howlet snatching up a bodger in the yard, as howlets sometimes do...

[*...are you all right?*]

[*I don't like stories where bodgers die. bodgers are cute.*]

[*how do you feel about razers?*]

[*okay, razers.*]

...told himself it was just a howlet snatching up a *razer* in the yard, as howlets sometimes do, and so he went to bed.

The next morning, he found razer fur in a neat circle around the epicenter. The rest of the razer was gone. A howlet could have done that, he supposed, but it *looked* like the circle with nothing in it had eaten the bodger.

[*razer!*]

...had eaten the razer.

Gangle decided to conduct some experiments. First, he found a nice round rock and placed it near the circle. And then he waited. Nothing happened to the rock for the rest of the day, but the *next* day the rock was gone.

He found a second rock and put it much closer to the ring, right on top of the razer fur.

He waited again. This time, the rock moved, gently at first before rolling steadily toward the epicenter.

Then the rock disappeared.

Was it magic? Gangle had lived his entire life in a world where there was no such thing as magic, and felt strongly that if that fact were to change, the change would come in a more compelling form than disintegrating rocks, skinned razers and confused plants. Therefore, he did not think it was magic.

However, he was unable to imagine an alternative explanation.

Possessed as he was of a mind that—while short on advanced scientific knowledge—had a basic grasp of the scientific *method*, Gangle decided to conduct further experiments.

His next test was to poke the epicenter with a long twig. He considered this to be a modest risk as compared to the rock test because he would be holding onto the other end of the stick, and so he took the precaution of wearing a rubber glove on his hand.

This would protect him if whatever was eating rocks and razers was electrical in nature, he reasoned. He didn't think it *was*, but he also couldn't rule it out.

What happened next was...nothing. At first. Gangle ran the tip of the stick through the middle and out the other side. The twig was neither devoured nor stripped of its outer layer or otherwise damaged.

Gangle pulled the stick back and tried again, only more slowly. This time, when the tip of the twig came close to the ring of dead grass, Gangle felt an ever-so-slight rightward tug. Loosening his grip, he allowed the twig to get pulled in that direction until it ran into... Gangle had no word for what it ran into. Something small but irrevocable. Something that atomized the twig at the intersection point, with the destruction causing a slight tremble down the length of the wood.

[*atomized?*]

[*destroyed. ate.*]

With some time and effort, he was able to relocate the precise point at which the twig met its doom, aimed the new tip *at* that point, and pushed forward until the only part of the twig remaining was what was in Gangle's hand.

Gangle tried it again with another twig and achieved the same result. Then he went inside and spent the rest of the day conducting research.

Once he'd finished his research he arrived at a conclusion that was a very *good* conclusion, except that it was obviously impossible. However, it was slightly *less* impossible than the notion that this was a magical event and so he decided it must be correct.

That conclusion was this: he had a tiny quantum singularity in his garden.

[*did you make that up?*]

[*did I make what up?*]

[*quantum singularity.*]

[*no.*]

[*that sounds like something you made up.*]

[*I didn't make it up.*]

[*okay.*]

Gangle knew he had to tell somebody about this problem, but wasn't sure who. There were well-established channels available for reporting things like downed trees and dead animals, but there was no municipal department in charge of rogue singularities. Still, he felt certain *someone* in City Hall would know what to do, and so he went there to ask. This did not go well.

The first person he spoke to didn't know what a quantum singularity was. She transferred him to her supervisor who *also* didn't know what a quantum singularity was but was certain if Gangle *had* one it was definitely a zoning violation. Gangle asked him to identify what *law* the private ownership of a quantum singularity was breaking, and after the better part of an afternoon's worth of searching, the man agreed that there was no such law on the books. He then added that there *should* be, and vowed to ensure one would be there in the future.

Once that was settled, Gangle returned to the question of what he should *do* about the singularity. The official sent him to the waste disposal department. They were not helpful.

Gangle concluded that City Hall was *not* where to go to find someone who knew what to do about a singularity in a garden. He would try the university instead.

After a little work he managed to find a physics professor named Cole. She *did* know what a singularity was, but also asserted—with great conviction—that he couldn't possibly have one in his yard.

"Micro singularities are *possible*," she explained, "but they are unstable. It would blink out of existence in a fraction of a second."

"What if they were not?" Gangle asked. "What if we were wrong about that? What if there *is* one in my garden?"

Cole laughed. "Then we will all be in great trouble, because the only thing a stable singularity can do is grow into a black hole. This would ultimately consume the planet, for black holes will always eat."

[*ohhhhh.*]

[*what is it?*]

[*singularities are black holes. I've heard of black holes.*]

Not laughing at all, Gangle asked, "how long do you think we have? Before that happens?"

"There is no telling, because nobody has ever created a stable micro singularity that lasted long enough to measure such a thing, nor would anyone want to do so. But it is an interesting question, and now I would like to know the answer to this as well. I will do the calculations. Come back in a month and I will tell you."

"Does this mean you believe me?" he asked hopefully.

"Absolutely not, but it is an interesting thought experiment."

In the month that followed the singularity did indeed grow, if only a little. More of the grass was dying around the epicenter, there was now a visible depression in the middle, and when Gangle stood nearby he could *feel* a gentle sideways tug. Also—and this may have been a coincidence—it seemed as if there was a marked increase in the number of missing pets in the neighborhood.

Gangle tried new experiments.

- He put a clock on the ground next to the singularity to see if it ran more slowly. He saw no change, but the clock only counted down to seconds, whereas any difference would probably have to be measured in microseconds. He declared this test inconclusive.
- He poured fine-grained sand over the epicenter to see if that helped pinpoint the singularity, thinking it reasonable to expect a few of the grains to enter into a tiny orbit. This was a qualified success, because while he failed to add a satellite to the miniature black hole, he did see a spark of light from when some of the grains touched the singularity's event horizon.
- He took a large metal can and put it over the singularity. This was in part for the benefit of the neighborhood pets who had not *yet* gone missing and in part because he wanted to see what would happen to the can. What happened was, the can began to dent slightly. It made loud noises when the

dents formed, at all hours, so he removed the can after a few days rather than see the experiment to its conclusion.

At the end of the month, as Gangle prepared to travel back to the university to once again try convincing Professor Cole that he really did have a singularity in his garden, she showed up at his front door, along with a man Gangle did not know.

After apologizing for the unannounced visit, Cole introduced the man as an industrialist named Xybax.

"I finished my calculations two weeks ago," Cole said, in what sounded like an explanation for the two of them being there, but which was not. "This is only a rough estimate, because I lack adequate numbers on initial conditions, but assuming the singularity was *just* created, we have anywhere between seven and a hundred years."

"That is indeed a rough estimate," Gangle said.

"I know. Which is why I reached out to Industrialist Xybax for advice on a more exact estimate."

"I have a supercollider," Xybax said, which meant very little to Gangle. "With it I have studied micro singularities."

"And did you?" Gangle asked. "Get a better number?"

"We did not," Xybax said. "But then I asked Cole *why* she wanted one and she told me about you. I agreed with her; micro singularities are rare and unstable and it's impossible for you to have one in your garden."

"However," Cole added, "we believe you *do* have one."

Xybax continued. "Since we thought it such a curious question—and since Cole insisted you were in possession of an otherwise sensible demeanor—we decided to conduct an aerial survey. What we learned was that your yard is too massive."

"Does this prove that I am correct?" Gangle asked.

"It might," Cole said.

"May we *see* your garden?" Xybax asked.

Gangle brought them to the garden. As a solitary person, Gangle had always looked forward to the day in which he could bring around important people to have a look at his flowers, as he was quite proud of them. But they weren't interested in his flowers.

[*aww. they should tell him his flowers are nice.*]

"What lovely flowers you have," Cole said, on her way to the singularity.

[*thank youuuu.*]

After conducting a number of tests to further confirm that, indeed, Gangle had a tiny black hole in his yard, Xybax said, quite unexpectedly, "I would like to purchase your singularity."

This was an odd thing to say. In approaching Professor Cole —and City Hall before her—Gangle had hoped for a resolution that involved making the singularity go *away*, i.e., dissolving it somehow. *Selling* it had never been a consideration.

"I don't understand," Gangle said. "Do you mean to purchase my garden as well? And my home?"

"We will *extract* it from the yard," Xybax said, "but we have to act quickly before it grows so massive as to make it impossible to move."

"But you are going to *destroy* it, yes? My understanding of singularities is not as great as Professor Cole's but I feel certain *keeping one around* is dangerous. As she said, black holes will always eat."

"It cannot be destroyed," Cole said.

"We mean to study it," Xybax said. "For you see, it *should* be impossible; that it is *not* makes it something worthy of study.

And my facility has all the means to conduct such an investigation."

"And *then* you will...not destroy, but get rid of it? Before it grows too large? You could put it on a rocket and launch it into space, while it is still small enough to fit on a rocket."

"Yes," Xybax said. "This is a very good idea. Thank you. We will do exactly that."

The singularity was removed the following day, as was very nearly the entire garden and most of the soil. Xybax's team lifted the space surrounding the singularity from the yard and dropped it into a large magnetic containment field that was a section of a supercollider a week earlier. Then they left.

Gangle was well-compensated; *so* well, he moved to a better house with a larger yard. Then he went to work on a *new* garden.

And he waited for news. He assumed there would eventually be an announcement of a rocket being sent into space carrying a dangerous payload of some sort. Rockets sent into outer space were uncommon and typically newsworthy, and furthermore impossible to keep a secret.

Yet there was no news. And so, after many months, Gangle contacted Xybax about his concerns. Rather than *answer* those concerns, the industrialist invited Gangle to come for a visit.

Gangle arrived at Xybax Corporation's main facility the following morning, where he was met at the door by none other than Xybax himself. He brought Gangle directly into a massive room featuring—to Gangle's horror—a much larger version of his garden singularity.

"Is it not beautiful?" Xybax asked.

Gangle thought it was not in fact beautiful at all.

"I don't understand," Gangle said. "Are you *feeding* it?"

"Controlled growth. We're monitoring it carefully."

"Will you still be able to send it away on a rocket?"

Xybax laughed. "No, why would we ever do *that?* Gangle, you do not appreciate what we have here. Imagine a future that runs on an inexhaustible supply of clean energy! Energy that's actually a net *positive* for the environment!"

"I don't understand."

"We are feeding it a strict diet of trash; enormous truckloads of garbage from all over the world. Next month we start work on the stockpiles of nuclear waste. Your singularity is getting rid of all of it for us."

"But how is this an energy source?"

"With a very clever engine turns the gravitational power into an electrical source. Professor Cole designed it herself. In time, the *entire power grid* will be supported by what goes on in this room. And that is just the beginning. Once we have built it out the entire *planet's* energy can come from right here! This is a *very* exciting time!"

Gangle thought Xybax was perhaps insane, as this was far too much enthusiasm for someone talking about an object that could devour the planet. Either that, or Gangle was missing something.

"Professor Cole said it was impossible to destroy the singularity," he said.

"Yes, this is so."

"And you have no intention of launching it into space."

"It is already too late to do such a foolish thing. It is too massive now. No rocket on the planet has sufficient thrust to achieve escape velocity with that aboard."

"And it can only *grow*, is this not correct? It cannot shrink."

"Actually, it can," Xybax said. "But only in the vacuum of space, absent fuel, and over a vast period of time. So yes, for the purposes of our current circumstance, it can only grow."

"Then will it not eventually consume us all?" Gangle asked. "Or have I overlooked an alternative."

Xybax smiled. "It will not be a problem for *us*. Nor for our children, our children's children, or our children's children's children. Our children's children's children's children's children's children's children may have some difficulty but of course by then it will hardly matter."

"Why is that?"

Xybax put his hand on Gangle's shoulder and turned him to face the singularity. "*Look* at it, Gangle. You are focusing on its destructive potential, but that is not what *I* see at all! *I* see a utopian future built on the harnessing of this great force. Surely, in *that* future they will figure out how to resolve a problem that to us, right now, *appears* impossible to solve. Have faith in the cleverness of our descendants, Gangle."

[...]

[*...why did you stop?*]

[*I'm not sure of the ending for this one.*]

[*stories have happy endings, daddy.*]

[*do they? always?*]

[*daaaaaddy...*]

[*all right.*]

Gangle returned home, concerned but also confident that a man as smart as Xybax must surely have superior insight into matters such as this.

And in the years that followed, Xybax's idealized vision did indeed come true: the planet was cleaner, energy was cheap and plentiful, and everyone was happy.

The end.

———

"NO, NO, NO," Celi said. "That's not the right ending at *all*."

"What ending were you hoping for?"

"Gangle should have convinced Xybax that he was *wrong* and to get *rid* of the singularity like he was supposed to."

"But it was too late for that," Pyrish said. "Xybax said it was already too large to send away."

"Then change that part of the story!"

"Then it would be a *different* story, wouldn't it?"

Celi frowned. "But-but-but *then* what happened? Will their children's children's children's children's children's children's children's children be to be all right?"

Pyrish smiled. "I'll tell *their* story another time. Now you need to get some sleep."

"Fine."

He tucked her in, kissed her forehead and turned off the light.

"Daddy?" Celi said, when he was at the door. "They *will* be okay, right?"

"Who will?"

"Their children's children's you know. You don't have to tell me the whole story. I just want to know."

"Yes. A great many years in the future, the descendants of Xybax and Gangle work out a way to shrink the singularity so that it will *never* grow uncontrollably and destroy the planet. And everyone was fine."

"Okay. Good night, daddy."

"Good night, Celi."

Pyrish drifted back into the living pod and refilled his glass of whisky. Then he sat in the dark and stared at the lights of the city in the distance. They had a good view of the downtown from their little home on the hill, a view that included the massive central Facility building.

The launch pad on the far end of the city usually offered a lightshow of rockets at this time of night too—one every few minutes—but those had mostly stopped. They hadn't run out of rockets; just people who could afford them.

Pyrish sighed. He was expected back at the Facility in a few hours, and it would be better if he arrived sober. Not that it would matter all that much if he was; it wouldn't change anything. But there was a matter of keeping up appearances, not causing a panic and so forth.

He kept drinking.

There was a great rumble in the distance. It came from the Facility, which had been making alarming noises for months now. Pyrish was one of the only people left who knew *why*.

The Source had breached containment. Like all the other times this had happened, there was still a chance they'd be able to get it back under control before it reached the absolute point of no return. But they would only be buying themselves a few weeks, because all they had left was short-term solutions, and they would eventually run out of those too.

Black holes will always eat. And there was nothing Pyrish could do to change that.

TRIBULATIONS OF LESSER MOON GODS

"I'm going to the moon," Yyamo said one late afternoon, absent prompting. "Will you come?"

She said this to Jezwe on the same day the moonrock man came, which should have been a memorable enough occasion on its own. But many seasons later, when Jezwe thought back to that day, it was this odd proclamation that came to mind first.

Not to discount the significance of the moonrock man's visit. Jezwe's father, Dongau, had been the local astroseer since their little fishing collective was barely ten families strong, clinging to the rocky shore of the southern edge of the Great Lake. Now, they were a burgeoning village, practically a metropolitan center like the pre-flood places of old... so large, the need for a properly consecrated observatorium seemed self-evident.

Still, it was ten years' worth of petitions to the village prelates, before they consented to raise sufficient barter to engage an honest moonrock man.

"Of course you are, "Jezwe said, with a laugh. "How do you mean to get there?"

Yyamo was possessed of a flat kind of humor that was

missed by all but a few; this was surely one of those times when she was being too subtle for even her best friend to detect.

"I'll take old Bunbrow's fishing boat," she said.

"To the moon."

"As I said."

Jezwe took Yyamo by the shoulders, put his finger under her chin, and tilted her head skyward. "This moon," he said, directing her attention to the fat moon on the horizon. "The moon in the sky."

"Yes, yes, yes, that moon, in that sky. I am taking a fishing boat to the moon, and I am asking you to come. I do not want to go alone, and when I get there I do not want to *be* alone."

She *was* serious, but then, perhaps she could afford to be. When one made one's mind up to do something impossible, fortitude was easy to come by. He could declare an intent to levitate, spend his life working at it stridently, and never succeed. Yyamo simply had a challenging day on the lake, and had decided she was finished with this world.

"All right," Jezwe said. "I'll go to the moon with you. Only Bunbrow will be upset that you've stolen his boat."

"Bunbrow can choke. The boat is more mine than his anyway."

THE MOONROCK MAN'S name was Stovis, a skinny outsider clothed in baggy animal hide, heavy leather boots, and a brimmed canvas hat. He had a chain around his neck with a seeing lens on a loop over a stiff white collar, marking him as an astroseer of the same order as Seer Dongau. He reeked of sweat and rendered animal fat, but was otherwise a charming dinner guest.

Stovis told long, dramatic tales of distant lands Jezwe never expected to see: great cities hung on the skeletons of pre-flood empires; a walled enclave built around the largest observatorium in the land; saltwater flat spearfishermen astride floating villages; small tribes stalking hooved animal herds on grassy steppes; vertical collectives thriving in carved dugouts on the wall of a glacier. Stovis traveled up and down the countryside along an east-west trade route called the Naifai, in a horse-pulled wagon, delivering goods from where they were plenty to where they were scarce. Moonrocks were hardly his only business.

"And here it is!" Stovis declared, after two helpings of whitefish and boiled greens. Opening his satchel, Stovis extracted an ornate wooden box, archaic lettering carved into the lid. He set the box on the table before Dongau, with a quick astroseer gestural blessing: fingers curled under the thumb, pressed to the heart. "As we see, so are we seen," he said.

"As we see, so are we seen," Dongau replied, opening the box. Jezwe, unable to rein in his curiosity, stood behind his father's chair to get a look at the rarest of the rare.

It was...a rock. Just a rock, no larger than a robin's egg. Smooth in some places and jagged in others, it neither shined nor sparkled. There were hundreds of thousands of examples of similar rocks right outside the window. The shore of the Great Lake was replete with them.

His father raised it from the box, slowly, gently, as if it actually *was* a robin's egg. "It's magnificent," he said, holding it in the light, where it continued to perform a spectacular job of being a rock. "Thank you, Seer Stovis."

"How does one acquire such a rock?" Jezwe asked.

"Jezwe..." Dongau muttered.

"I only mean to understand how one can tell. Did the gods deliver this to you directly?"

"Please forgive my son," Dongau said. "He is on another path."

"Not at all, Seer Dongau," Stovis said. To Jezwe, he asked, "have you not studied?"

"This is a question to a question, good sir," Jezwe said. "I am not a novitiate, but yes, I have studied."

"Recall, there are places where the gods *used* to live, before this world drowned in their wrath. I know these places. So does your father. And so would *you*, if you took the oath."

"These places are beneath the waters, are they not?" Jezwe asked.

"They are," Stovis said, "which is why such a fee is attached to my services. Finding and retrieving moonrocks is no simple matter. They're not discovered just lying about on the ground."

Jezwe thought that was precisely how Stovis had come across this unspectacular moonrock of his, but did not say so. He had already pushed his father's patience.

"No offense intended, Seer Stovis," Jezwe said. "I thank you for answering my questions."

After Dongau saw Stovis to the door, he returned to Jezwe, a sour look on his face. "You come with me tonight," he said.

THE DEVICE WAS CALLED A LUNASCOPE. It was little more than a column of lenses in a tube, affixed to a tripod, but for the believers in the Great Lake shoreline congregation—for whom Seer Dongau was their only direct conduit to the gods—it was the epicenter of the faith.

Now that Dongau had secured a moonrock, the new observatorium's foundation could be laid. Then the building— rounded walls, a domed roof—would go up, and then? The installation of a proper lunascope.

The old 'scope, a fussy antique in constant need of repair, was nearing the end of its life cycle. But it wasn't done for yet. And so, as it was with every other cloudless night, Dongau carried the old thing to the top of Galgot Hill, assembled it, and made his observations.

As a boy, Jezwe would accompany his father up that hill most every night, begging all the while for a chance to use it himself. Always, the answer was no.

"You are too young," Dongau would say. "And you've not prepared."

Jezwe was now old enough, but with puberty came doubt, which led to his stopping short of taking the oath of the novitiate. He therefore remained unprepared to look through the eye of the lunascope.

It had been many years since he'd climbed the hill with his father; this was the first time he could recall Dongau not only asking but *insisting*. Thinking the other option was a beating, Jezwe assented.

They set up the lunascope in silence. Then Dongau pulled out his notebook, aimed the glass at the moon, and began the long process of focusing.

"Tell me about this friend of yours," Dongau said, as he worked. "The lungfisher."

"Yyamo? What is there to tell?"

His father looked up, a slight smile visible in the starlight. "That is for *you* to say, not me."

"Oh," Jezwe said, blushing. "We are not like that. I don't think... I don't believe she considers me in that way. Not with..."

Jezwe put his hand to the scars on the left side of his face, as the rest of his answer.

"That's an excuse," Dongau said.

"I accept that my disfigurement renders me undesirable," Jezwe said. "It's not an excuse."

"Since the fire, child, you have fallen on your scars as an explanation for all you do, and all you don't. You wonder why I ask after the girl; it's not because she's an able match. She's *not*, may I add. You are the learned son of an astroseer; she is an indentured lungfisher, beneath you in station. But if you had intentions, I would not interfere. Not if she makes you happy."

He looked up from the eyepiece.

"But nothing makes you happy, Jezwe. I see that, even if you don't. I *ask*, because on the day her indenture is ended, she will be *skilled* in something. The only position you have trained for is astroseer, except that your only true *skill* is doubt. My hope is that my only living child realizes his potential, and enjoins it with a profession that will keep him fed. Failing that, perhaps he will stumble upon a partner capable of feeding him."

"Such as Yyamo," Jezwe said.

"I promise, of the two, you are the only one who still sees the scars. Now come here and look."

Dongau stepped back from the eyepiece.

"I can't use that," Jezwe said. "It's not allowed."

"I am your astroseer, and I say it *is* allowed. Go on. You've always wanted to."

"Very well," Jezwe said, stepping forward.

It had always been possible to see the city of the gods with the naked eye, but with none of the detail: lights along gridlines, a vague hint of structures, and so on. Enough to support a faith. But the knowledge of the finer details—and, more importantly, the correct *interpretation* of those details—was reserved for the astroseers.

Or so they said. This was Jezwe's cardinal doubt. As he matured, and it became obvious anyone with access to focusing lenses could look at the city as closely as an astroseer, he began to wonder if there was any real difference between the "correct" interpretation and the "heretical musings" of the uninitiated. To him, they both sounded like guesses. The astroseers just had more historical texts to fall back on.

As for what that detail *was*, until this moment Jezwe could only speculate.

He pressed up against the eyepiece and got his first real look at the city of the gods.

It was extraordinary: ornate spires of white stone; domed buildings spread across the surface, connected by long, black corridors; a *lake* sparkling in the starlight; silvery ground-level capstones in what, for the moon, would qualify as an open field; a huge glass building with *plants* on one side; all of it ringed by candles that burned without flame.

It was easy to see how someone looking upon this would fall back on *gods* as an explanation. Who but the gods would live like this?

"It's glorious," Jezwe said. "I can see why you find this so fascinating."

Dongau laughed. "We are subjects of the gods, and answer to their whims. This is no hobby."

"Gods we cannot see. Unless I have simply failed to notice one."

"Oh, they are there."

Jezwe was about to offer a rejoinder—something sharp, but not so much so as to initiate a new argument—when one of the capstones in the field disappeared.

No, that was not correct. It didn't disappear; it opened. It was a lid atop a hole in the moon.

Something needle-shaped slid out of the hole and shot straight up from the surface.

Jezwe gasped. "What is *that?*" he asked.

Dongau nudged him aside to look for himself. "A gift," he said, quickly refocusing the apparatus to track the object rocketing away from the moon.

"A gift?"

"Indeed. The gods have sent a fire dragon, and you've had the rare fortune of bearing witness; consider yourself blessed."

"YOU SAW NO GODS?" Yyamo asked. "This is disappointing."

"You *would* focus on that," Jezwe said.

It was frankly impossible to convey the splendor that was the city of the moon gods, using only words. (Or, it was impossible for *Jezwe*, who was no poet.) But he thought his description of the *impact* it had on him, an avowed doubter, would have moved her.

It had not.

"But the lake is there," she said. "Just as in the teachings. Good. I will need a place for the boat."

Jezwe laughed. He was still waiting for Yyamo to admit she was joking.

"The part with the fire dragon was interesting," she added. "A needle, you say?"

"That's what it looked like."

She looked skyward. "I wonder when it spreads its wings."

A full day had passed since Jezwe's witnessing of the dragon's launch. According to his father, in his position as Seer Dongau for the Great Lake villages, they could expect it to reach them sometime between midday and moonrise; all should prepare accordingly.

This meant making sure everyone was off the lake, turning the occasion into an informal holiday—Dragon Day—for this tribe of fishers. Families held celebrations all along the shore, and Dongau's schedule was frenetic, as everyone of import demanded his attention, wisdom and blessing. This left Jezwe with nothing but free time; he chose to spend it with Yyamo.

They were sitting in Bunbrow's fishing boat, which had been dragged from the water a few hours earlier, after Yyamo had completed an early morning fishing expedition.

The boat still smelled of fish. Unless that was her. She'd changed out of the dive suit—now drying atop a steel lung further ashore—and was clothed in only the skin-tight under-layer. Jezwe felt overdressed.

Yyamo reached around the side of the boat to grab another bottle of cider. "Look at them," she said, nodding to the shore parties taking place in both directions. "You would think they had never seen a dragon before."

"It's been, what, two seasons?" Jezwe said.

"The last Great Lake dragon was only five moons ago," Yyamo said. "What you mean to say, this is the first in two seasons for which your father has given adequate notice. He's faltering."

"He's *not*. His lunascope can't penetrate the clouds, or see the moon by day. He can only do so much."

"You're too easy to tease," Yyamo said with a laugh. She handed him a bottle. "Here. Drink more, and stop taking everything so seriously."

Jezwe grumbled, but took the cider. "It's not his fault, I only mean to say."

"Yes, yes, yes."

They sat in silence, drinking and staring at the cloudless afternoon sky for a while.

There was no telling exactly when the fire dragon would appear; they only knew the day, not the hour. They could be waiting until well after sunset. As aggravating as it was to sit for that long, Jezwe secretly hoped for a nighttime arrival, which was far more spectacular.

"He doesn't have to build an entire observatorium, if his only goal is to better detect fire dragons," Yyamo said, after a time. "He can just ask me."

"You," Jezwe said. "The most faithless soul in the village."

"I wouldn't say I'm *without* faith. Just not in the gods. You feel the same, whether you're able to confess it or not; I wouldn't care for you otherwise. But yes, I can tell Seer Dongau when to expect another dragon; he only need ask."

"How would *you* know?"

"I'm not going to tell you," she said. "But it's hardly a secret. The lungfishers know."

Any further probing on this point would have to wait, because the siren went off then; one of the spotters had seen it.

"Here we go," Yyamo said.

High up in the cloudless sky, a tease of flame from the east, visible to the naked eye but not *obvious*. Had they not known where to look, they'd have missed it.

There was a murmur of activity up and down the shore, as the aggregated dragon-watch parties backed up the beach. Jezwe and Yyamo stayed where they were, because the wave was supposed to be part of the experience.

The pinhole of light grew to a ball of flame, and then a ball of flame with extended wings. It seemed to take forever to reach the lake, until all at once it was there: a huge, red-hot dragon with a massive gaping mouth, a hide of shimmering steel, and fiery wings to help guide it in.

The dragon plummeted straight into the water, which hissed and shrieked. A giant plume of steam shot up from the wound.

Then came a terrible silence.

Ten, fifteen, twenty seconds passed—it always seemed twice as long as it ought to be—before the dragon emerged from the depths again, aimed straight for the heavens. It closed its mouth as soon as it was out of the water, its wings shifted, and a great flame burst from its tail.

The climb away from the surface of the lake began so slowly that the dragon seemed, at times, to not be moving at all. Would the dragon make it back to the sky? Or *this* time, for the first time ever, would it fall back down again?

Then the pace picked up, and the crowd—exhaling collectively—gave a cheer, as it roared upward.

The wave came next. While the dragon's impact on the surface of the lake created a wave of its own, it was nothing compared to what happened when the full force of the tail flame hit the water.

"Ohh, this will be a good one," Yyamo said, as a wall of water twice her height raced to the shore. She grabbed both sides of the boat, eyes forward, as if daring the wave to knock her over.

To the rest of the crowd, the fire dragon was a blessing from the moon gods; for Yyamo, it was the *wave* that was the blessing.

Jezwe's approach was decidedly more relaxed: he pulled the bottles of cider into the boat and huddled down over them. This was no blessing; it was just a way to end up wet.

The water crashed ashore, pummeling Yyamo—shouting, when she should have been holding her breath—and Jezwe. The boat they were sitting in was carried backwards several paces.

Jezwe remained huddled over the bottles until it was over, then sat up to see the water receding. Yyamo looked at him and shook her head.

"Gods," she said. "This would be easier if you swam."

"*What* would be easier?"

"No matter. Let's go drink."

"I AM GOING to get you on a lung," Yyamo said. "It's decided."

"I've no interest in fishing," Jezwe said. "Or in fish, beyond the dinner table."

"Hah! Not fishing, *gods*, not fishing. Your talent lies in opening and closing books, Jezwe. I mean to take you under the lake as a *guest*. You only need to flounder about. Please tell me Dongau's lessons included floundering about in deep water."

"I know how to swim. I don't enjoy it."

"Then you don't *really* know how to swim," Yyamo said.

"The same could be said of you," Jezwe said, "and reading."

"Not the same at all. *Nobody* enjoys reading. You only pretend to, to keep your father happy. And I don't know how to read."

"I haven't made him happy in years. You know this."

"I do," she said, getting to her feet. "But you still try. Another round."

"None for me," Jezwe said.

"Wasn't a question."

It had been hours since they'd left the shore of the Great Lake, and relocated to Sill's Pub. The family-friendly portion of Dragon Day carousing ended not long after nightfall, as did the many ceremonies entreating the gods to smile upon their servants, now that they had exacted tribute.

With the responsible adults and the devout—often, but not always, the same subset—retired for the night, it was up to the childless, the young, and the otherwise irresponsible to carry the celebration into morning.

Yyamo pushed her way to the bar, and signaled the need for two fresh bottles by slapping three coins on the bar top. She was now clothed in baggy overalls and a threadbare sweater, an outfit that identified her as a lungfisher just as clearly as the underlayer and dive suit. If there was pocket coin to be spent, it would go to what was worn *in* the water; for shore, better to have something warm and cheap that was loose enough to go over dive clothes.

Clothing-wise, Yyamo didn't stand out. Nor would she have had she *not* changed, as Sill's was a fisher's bar. Conversely, Jezwe—in clothing which, while still somewhat damp from the soaking at the shoreline, actually *fit* him—stuck out as possibly the only person in the place who didn't earn a living on the water.

Bottles in hand, Yyamo stumbled back to the table. "Next round is yours to buy," she said, putting the drinks down.

"I'm calling it after this," Jezwe said.

"Not while the sun's below the horizon, you..."

Whatever derogation that was to follow died in her throat, as someone had just entered the pub that she was clearly *not* happy to see. Jezwe turned to check the doorway, but he already knew who it was: old man Bunbrow, the only person on Ter who could engender such a malign expression from Yyamo.

"Hold," she said, to Jezwe. "He has no claim."

Bunbrow used to fish the lake himself, when he was young and fit. Now, the profits of his youth were buried in three boats run by indentured help; he spent most of his days walking the shore—on a cane, as his weight had conspired to ruin one of his knees—and complaining.

"There you are, girl," he growled, as the barroom got notably quieter. "There's *fish* to be caught in a few hours, yet here you sit."

"There's none to be *had*, you old fool," Yyamo spat back. "What fish the dragon didn't take will be hiding in the depths for another two days. Every fisher worth their lung knows this."

Bunbrow's response was to crack Yyamo across the face with the hook of his cane. She fell from the chair to her knees, and the entire room froze.

"If the fish are in the depths, then that is where you will go," Bunbrow said. "Now do as you're told and get to your bedroll."

Yyamo spat blood on the floor. "No," she said, raising her head slowly. "It's Dragon Day. I'm not going anywhere. We're celebrating."

Jezwe kept expecting another of the lungfishers to step in and interrupt this, but none looked interested in doing anything of the kind, so when Bunbrow raised his cane to strike Yyamo again, it was Jezwe who got in his way.

"Stop," Jezwe said. "She can't fish if her head is caved in, either."

Bunbrow lowered the cane and stared at him. "Or you'll stop me? You? A soft-handed shore-hugging little *boy*? Get out of my way, this is not your matter."

"No."

Bunbrow stepped closer, staring down at Jezwe with undisguised scorn. He smelled like a man rotting from the inside out.

"I *know* you," the old man said. "The astroseer's boy. Do the gods stand with you, child? Is that what you think?"

"I *think* there's no need for you to strike my friend," Jezwe said.

"Well! What *I* think is, had the fire that took half of your face and your mother's life *also* claimed the most holy Seer Dongau, then *perhaps* those thieving gods of his would fuck off and leave us alone. That is what *I* think. Now stand aside!"

"Again, no."

Bunbrow glared at Jezwe, a half beat away from turning the cane on him as well. But the consequence of striking the son of the astroseer was difficult to calculate, and so he relented. "On the water by sunrise," he said, staring at Jezwe but speaking to Yyamo, "or there will be consequences."

THEY WERE NO LONGER WELCOME in Sill's. This became obvious shortly after Bunbrow left, yet the barroom failed to return to its prior level of general carousing. It seemed that Yyamo, by taking a strike from a boatmaster on the premises, had violated some unspoken etiquette. Or perhaps it was Jezwe's mistake, for helping. Or, for being there at all.

Jezwe helped Yyamo to her feet—she expressed her dislike of this with a string of expletives—and together they left.

"It's all right," Jezwe said, as they staggered along the shore. On most nights, she bedded down in the unheated shack that also housed the fishing boat, which was where he was leading her.

"You should not have done that," she muttered.

"I will be all right," he said. "That old man doesn't frighten me."

"No," she said, pushing away from him. "This is not about *you*. He will take this out on *me*, how can you not see that?"

"He could have killed you, Yyamo..."

"He would have *stopped*. And tomorrow, when my boat came back empty, he would have given me the coin for a full haul anyway out of guilt. *I told you to hold!*"

"Nobody else was going to stop him..."

"Because they knew it would only make things worse! As *you* have done! Only, no. No, you've done more damage than any intervening fisher could *possibly* have, because now he knows the company I keep. I can hear him already. 'Don't cry when I short you, girl; ask your beloved for the coin.' Gods, you have set me back *so* far, Jezwe."

"But I'm not rich. And you and I, we're... we're not..."

"*It doesn't matter*, how do you not see that? And for *wealth*...? You truly have no idea, do you? Look past your scars, Seer Jezwe. You're missing the world."

"Don't call me that," he said.

"Go. I will find my own way back."

"But you can barely…"

"*Leave me alone.*"

She nearly fell over. He lunged forward to catch her, but she held up her hands. "I mean it," she said. "It would be best if you were not around."

"Then… all right, then I'll see you…"

"*At all*, Jezwe. Go have a life and leave me alone."

THE NEXT FEW months went poorly for Jezwe.

It was untrue, what Dongau said, about his prospects for a career. Jezwe could read both modern scratch and archaic pre-flood text; his father's inability to see this as a skill, with value outside of the faith, was Dongau's shortcoming, not Jezwe's.

Admittedly, it was difficult to see it as something on which to build a *career*; not in a small fishing village. But surely, were Jezwe to "go have a life," as Yyamo suggested, he would thrive in one of the great cities described by Stovis. There would always be archaic text in need of translating and—he assumed—plenty of persons of means interested in a translator not wearing the collar of an astroseer.

Or, he could tutor.

This was what he did with his free time, most days. The coin he earned mostly went toward their household costs, or to the observatorium building expenses, but some of it made its way into Jezwe's pocket.

He was already tutoring before Yyamo abruptly resigned from his life, and took on more students after, as a way to keep occupied until he figured out what to do about her. He never quite worked that out, which only made him irritable, and a decidedly less effective teacher.

Dongau, if he noticed at all, didn't say anything.

It all changed one morning, when Jezwe found a box outside his front door.

In the box, was a dive suit underlayer. It was his size.

———

HE FOUND Yyamo on the shore, packing Bunbrow's fishing boat with gear. She was in a dive suit he'd only seen a few times; it was a heavy rubber outfit, only slightly less skintight than the underlayer beneath it. From what little Jezwe understood about the mechanics of diving, the outer layer offset the compression (somehow) of the deeper waters in the lake, kept the lungdiver warm, and would even inflate to carry the wearer to the surface, in the event of something catastrophic. He was also told that effectively operating underwater in that kind of suit took one to two seasons' worth of training, in shallow water, under closely guided instruction.

He didn't know why *he* was there, or why he was currently wearing a dive suit underlayer beneath his regular clothes.

But, he was glad to see Yyamo.

"There you are," she said, as if they had a standing appointment. "Help me load the boat."

"Ah, hello?" he said. "How have you been, and what are we doing?"

"We're going out on the water." She looked him up and down. "Good, you're wearing it," she said.

"How can you tell?"

"Your stance," she said. She kept working as they talked, tying down various pieces of equipment that Jezwe couldn't put names to. "You look like something's up your ass. More than usual. Are you going to help, or not? I still have to load two more tanks."

"Can we talk first?" he asked.

"We'll talk on the water," she said. "Come on, we're on a tight schedule."

Jezwe looked down the coastline. All he saw was boats, and none on the water. "The urgency appears to be yours alone," he noted.

"We're expecting more rain," she said. "You would think after spending the day under the water, nobody would care if they got wet in the boat as well, but they do."

"But why the rush?"

She sighed, and stepped up to him. "All right," she said. "I am sorry, for what I said. I was tired, and drunk, and angry, but not at you."

"Thank you for saying so," he said. "And I'm sorry…"

"Forget it. Now let's go."

"But, I still don't…"

"Jezwe. I said one day I would teach you to dive. Today is that day. I know you want more than that, but it will have to wait until after we've finished loading the boat and pushed off. I promise, we will have plenty of time to talk. All right?"

He didn't want to go out on the water, and he *definitely* didn't want to go diving. But he also didn't want to lose out on reconnecting with Yyamo.

"I'll go out there," he said. "After that, no promises."

"You will change your mind," she said. "Now go get that lung and bring it here. Lift with your knees."

JEZWE KNEW ONLY the basic mechanics of lungfishing. Fishers like Yyamo would pick a location somewhere in the middle of the lake, strap on a lung, grab a net, and dive. If successful, they would emerge minutes or hours later with a full net. Then they'd either return to shore, or go down for more, depending on the size of the first haul, the time of day, and—he was sure—any number of other factors.

On the details, he was fuzzy. How did they know where to put the boat? He'd heard mention of "fish-finders," which were either electrical devices that used (presumably pre-flood) technology to locate schools of fish, or faith-based scrying tools, whose merit depended upon the user's belief in their value.

How deep did they actually dive, and how did they know where to *stop*? As he understood it, the lungfishers didn't *chase* fish beneath the surface; they remained still, spread their nets, and waited for a school. Surely there was a *tell* of some sort down there, something to signify they'd reached some invisible fish thoroughfare. But he couldn't imagine what that might be.

Really, given the size and depth of the Great Lake, it seemed remarkable that they *ever* caught enough fish in a day to fill up a boat.

So he *was* curious. Just not curious enough to go underwater.

There didn't appear to be anything on the boat that qualified as a fish finder. There was also, by his count, four times as many lungs as needed. And only one net.

Yyamo rowed the boat out to a precisely-chosen spot in the middle of the lake that looked about the same as any other spot in the middle of the lake, and dropped anchor.

"Perfect," she said, checking the boat's location from several angles. "Now get those clothes off."

"I told you, I'm not going to dive," he said. "But I am happy to be out here with you, and I do have many questions about lungfishing."

She nodded. "You'll get answers to many of your questions today. Just not the questions you were expecting to have answered. And you will not dive today. I'll still need you to get out of those clothes and into the suit in the box you're sitting on."

She was preparing one of the lungs as she spoke. There was an odd urgency to her action; was she concerned she'd miss the fish?

"If I am not diving, why do I need a suit?" he asked, reasonably.

"Because you will still need to breathe."

"I am breathing just fine."

She sighed. "You are going to be difficult about this. All right. Here is one of your questions answered. Do you recall my boast that I can better guess a dragon's arrival than your father? You wanted to know how. Here is how: the fish know."

Jezwe laughed. He was imagining a trout with a lunascope. "And the fish tell *you*?" he asked.

"Their behavior changes. Something at the bottom of this lake drives the deep swimmers up to the floor of the warm current. The dragon arrives two days later."

"You're serious."

"I am. Now take off the clothing. You will need to be ready."

"Ready for...?"

All at once, Jezwe understood. The lack of other boats on the water; the curious fact that the Great Lake fish are in communion with the gods of the moon; Yyamo's insistence that he will need to *breathe* even if he doesn't *dive*.

And it has been overcast all week, he thought.

"A dragon is coming," Jezwe said.

"Very soon," she said. "You will have to hurry."

"Yyamo... no. No, this is madness. We have to get off the water."

"It's too late to get off the water. Do you not understand where we *are* right now?"

"I can swim, then. I'll swim to shore."

"You won't make it. Gods, *I* wouldn't make it from here. I told you I meant to take Bunbrow's boat to the moon, Jezwe, and you promised you'd come with me. Today is the day."

"That you meant to do so in the belly of a *dragon* is a detail I very much would have liked to know ahead of time!"

"That would ruin the surprise," she said. "And you would never have agreed to it."

"I don't agree to it *now!*"

"Yes, but *now* it doesn't matter."

"Pull up the anchor. We can row back to shore."

There was a flash of light in the sky above the eastern shore. The dragon had fallen below the clouds. They had only minutes.

"Jezwe, listen to me," Yyamo said. "The first rule of lung-fishing is, never panic. Now, you know the mouth will still be open when the dragon rises up from the depths, and I have put this boat in the *exact center* of that mouth. We will be fine as long as we remain precisely where we are right now. But if we *panic*, and start to row, when the dragon emerges it will break us. Only, we *won't* be fine because *you* are going to drown if you don't get out of those clothes and into the dive suit under your ass, *right now.*"

"All right," he said, taking off his shirt. "All right, but we..." He took another look at the dragon, growing larger far too quickly. "Gods. Okay."

He got out of his pants, turned around and opened the box to find... an entirely different dive suit than anything he'd ever seen before.

"What is this?"

"It's a deep sea pressure suit. We use them to explore the floor."

"Why don't I have the same thing *you* have?"

"Because *my* suit is for skilled lungfishers. *That* suit is for hapless lumps."

He picked out the helmet and tried it on. There was a small window in the front to see out of, but the rest of it was metal.

"That goes on last," Yyamo said.

He pulled the suit out next. It was a one-piece, with metal boots and thick gloves. "It's all so heavy," he said.

"Again, it's for walking on the bottom of the lake."

He slipped into the suit from an opening in the back, and then had to stand still while Yyamo sealed him in.

The dragon hit the far end of the lake.

"Gods, this will be close," Yyamo muttered. She pushed Jezwe down to his knees and strapped a lung onto his back, then went to work fastening it to whatever apparatus was built into the suit for air flow.

The wake of the dragon's entry hit them broadside then, and nearly took Jezwe right over the side.

"Done!" Yyamo said. She stumbled across the rocking deck and grabbed the helmet, slammed it down over his head, and turned it one quarter. He heard a lock engage, and air hissing.

"I can breathe," he said. "I can..."

Then the world erupted.

The dragon rose up from directly beneath the boat, surrounding them on all sides. For a heartbeat, it seemed as though they would continue that way, atop the water in a small tidepool at the tip of the dragon's maw. Then he felt wood shatter beneath his feet, the daylight disappeared, and he was pushed underwater by a great downward force.

Jezwe couldn't see or hear anything, and the rapid upward propulsion that would take the dragon away from the planet Ter was such that he couldn't really breathe either.

Yyamo never got to her lung, he thought. Then he blacked out.

IN THE PERFECT darkness of the dragon's belly, there was very little separating awake from not. Jezwe could barely move, whether his eyes were opened or closed there was nothing to see, and he couldn't feel anything; not even the pressure of motion.

He had perhaps been conscious for some time, and not realized. Were it not for the air moving through his lungs, he would have found an argument that he was *dead* compelling.

I am dead, he thought. *My body just hasn't caught up.*

It was roughly a day's travel to the moon. The lung on his back held less than a day's worth of oxygen. He didn't know where the spare lungs were, because it was perfectly dark and he couldn't move anyway, and if he *did* get his hands on another lung, he wouldn't know how to connect it to the suit.

And so, he was dead.

He wondered about Dongau. Would he find out what happened to his son? Surely, someone ashore saw what happened to Bunbrow's fishing boat and the two lunatics sitting in it. (Well, one lunatic, and one fool.) What would Dongau say, to his congregants? To himself?

When a housefire claimed the life of Dongau's wife and only daughter, *Seer* Dongau claimed—publicly and privately— that this was the will of the gods. Would he see this the same way? Or would he recognize it as the will of Yyamo, a stubborn, illiterate lungfisher with a stupid plan that didn't even include making sure she was wearing a lung when it came time to not drown?

"Damn you, Yyamo," he said. "Why did you leave me?"

An eternity in silence and blackness followed. He may have been unconscious again.

And then: a flash of light. Movement. Were his eyes open? Or was this what happened when one died?

No. It was a luminescent stick, in the hand of the surprisingly not-dead Yyamo.

As she swam closer with the light, Jezwe noticed a number of details about his surroundings he could not before. First, there were fish *everywhere*. Thousands, swimming in tight circles around both of them, as terrified as Jezwe with the sudden adjustment to the local reality. Second, the dragon's belly was *vast*. He couldn't see its walls. But—and this was third—he *could* see the floor, as he was lying atop it on his back. The shattered remains of the fishing boat lay all around him... including the spare lungs.

Yyamo swam up, pressed the front of her air mask against the glass of his helmet, and spoke. The vibrations traveled through the two pieces of headgear: crude, but sufficient.

"Get up, lazy," she said.

THEIR ARRIVAL WAS ABRUPT, but not unexpected; when the dragon slowed, they could feel it. Soon, they could also feel gravity pulling them downward toward the mouth. Then the belly's entire contents was disgorged, with some measure of violence, into a narrow, knee-deep canal.

To Jezwe, it felt a little like a rebirth, both for the literal process of ejection from a larger body, and for having previously thought of himself as dead.

He was carried halfway down the canal by the rush of water, ending up face-down and not entirely willing to move. He missed the part where the dragon closed its maw, and slid back out of the bladder that kept the canal from direct exposure to the atmosphere-free surface.

He was starved. He was exhausted. He was *alive*, but that was surely conditional.

Yyamo reached him, knocked on his helmet, pulled him to the edge of the canal. Then she looked him in the eye, took a deep breath, and removed her air mask. She took two deep breaths of moon air, and smiled.

Jezwe took off his helmet next, with some help from Yyamo.

"You are insane," was the first thing he had to say. It came after several sharp breaths. There was a vaguely acrid smell to the air on the moon.

"I expected something far less kind from you, Jezwe," she said. Yyamo looked happier than he had ever seen her, a condition she affirmed by abruptly kissing him on the mouth. "Now, let's get you out of this suit."

"Hungry," he said. "I'm very hungry."

The wood fragments of Bunbrow's boat had been carried down the canal along with the fish and all of the water, but its heavier, non-buoyant contents were scattered around them. Yyamo hunted through the detritus, emerging with a steel box, inside of which was enough dried beef to last a week.

"I packed for everything," she said. "Now turn around so I can unfasten that. We eat, and then we go to meet your gods."

THEY WALKED down the now-dry canal, to the shore of the very lake Jezwe witnessed through the eye of Dongau's lunascope, covered by a glass-paneled dome. This end of the 'scope featured a breathtaking vista of the planet Ter nestled in a starry night sky.

Yyamo dove straight into the water, emerging after a time a bit further down.

"It's full of fish!" she said. "We should find my net."

"We will have to ask the gods first," Jezwe said. "The fish belong to them now."

"Hah! We'll see. Meet you on the other shore."

There was an *orchard* on the far side of the lake: fruit-bearing trees with ripe apples and peaches and a number of other fruits Jezwe couldn't identify, spread out across a well-manicured lawn with brick pathways describing circuitous routes.

Yyamo plucked an apple from the nearest tree and took a bite before Jezwe could warn her against doing so.

"The apple belongs..."

"To the gods, I know," she said, tossing him the apple. "Let them come scold me, then. I have some choice words prepared. Take a bite; it's delicious. I wager it's your first taste of a fresh one. It's *mine*, certainly."

Jezwe bit into the apple. She was correct, in every regard. "I only caution against angering them preemptively," he said between bites. "We need their help to get back home. Assuming they don't execute us outright for our impertinence."

"Go *home?* Jezwe, look around! There could be nothing but piles of dung on the other side of this orchard and it would still be the most beautiful place I've ever seen. Why would you want to *leave?*"

"Yyamo, we can't *stay.*"

"You are incapable of happiness," she said. "That is your problem."

She marched off before he could concoct an effective rejoinder.

THE ORCHARD LED to a grand pavilion, the white spires he'd seen from afar looming overhead, visible through an elegant crystalline roof. This was a central choke point for transit, as a dozen corridors opened up onto the space. At its center was a grand altar, with a marble statue depicting some abstraction concerned with waves and lightning bolts.

According to the plaque, the piece was called *Day of Judging,* or something close to that. (The older the text, the more esoteric the verb forms, and this was very old text.)

The space was lit dimly by electrically powered floor lighting, which gave life to shadows, but nothing else. They remained alone, in a space designed for crowds.

Yyamo jumped onto the altar, cupped her hands around her mouth, and shouted, "*Hello?*"

Her words echoed back at them.

"It appears the gods have abandoned their city," she said.

"That isn't possible."

"You don't even *believe* in the gods."

"I have never professed any such thing," he said. "I have doubt. That's all."

"Your *doubt* has been supremely well-served today, Seer Jezwe."

"Don't call me that. And you?"

"I expected no gods, but also, I expected *someone*. Perhaps it is us. *We* are the gods of the moon."

"No."

"I see no other claimants."

"Then we can be lesser gods," he said. "For now. But it cannot *be* that there is no one else here."

She extended her arms and spun in a circle. "The conclusion may be *premature*, as the city is huge and they could be hiding, but does this feel like an occupied space to you?"

"Yet it cannot be," Jezwe said. "Not as a matter of faith, but logic. Someone tended to the trees, and the grass. The canonical record puts the great flood over four centuries past. That's four centuries of dragons restocking the moon lake with fish and water. Did the lake look overstocked to your eyes?"

"It didn't."

"The waters would have long ago crested the shore; we should be standing on fish carcasses right now. And ours is hardly the only tribute to the moon gods. Cattle, grains, beans, these are all offerings made to the gods from different parts of the world on different schedules. Four hundred years of consumption, Yyamo. Call the residents of this great city gods or not, but they *have* to be here."

"All right," Yyamo said. "Then let's find them."

JEZWE AND YYAMO spent the rest of the evening—if it *was* evening; how could one tell, on the moon?—exploring every corner of the city. What they found was marvel after marvel, as around each corner and through every passageway was the most extraordinary thing they'd ever seen, up until they turned the next corner or went down another passageway.

They found a massive vegetable garden; a below-ground coliseum with real grass, a ball field and a racetrack; an auditorium; a banquet hall with diamond chandeliers; a school; a museum with astonishing works of art; and many, many other spaces whose exact function eluded them both.

And there were the residences. The massive spires that loomed over the city appeared to be housing units, based on the spaces they examined on the second and third floors. This was also where they found the first *closed* doors in the entire facility. They initially appeared locked as well, but after holding his hand on the knob for a few moments, the locking mechanism disengaged and allowed entry.

Interestingly, this only worked once. Yyamo, at the same

door, could not open it. But the *next* unit's door opened for her, and *not* Jezwe. The technology behind the locks worked the same as a stray animal imprinting upon a new master, with the implication being that there was no longer a *prior* master to whom the doors answered.

The housing units were ornately decorated and highly personalized; it was clear that someone had lived there at one time. But not now.

It was in a particularly elegant second story unit—plush couches and chair, a bed twice the size of Bunbrow's shattered boat, a polished oak dining table, and a picture window with a glorious view of Ter on the moon's horizon—that they decided to rest, and reconsider.

"They left," Yyamo suggested.

"To where?" Jezewe asked.

"To wherever gods go. You tell me."

"But the food..."

"Yes, I accept your reasoning," she said. "But we've also not found any kitchens, or slaughterhouses. All we've seen is the front of the barroom; where's the filthy back room where the chickens are gutted and the ale is made?"

"Where is the filthy anything?" Jezwe asked. "All is gleaming and shiny."

"Perhaps there is no dust on the moon."

Yyamo's eyes drifted to a glass-and-metal panel on one of the walls. It was no different than the dozens upon dozens of other such panels in other parts of the city, and didn't serve any obvious function.

"What *are* these?" she asked, stepping up to it.

"I don't know," he said.

She put her hand on the panel; at once, light danced in the glass. She gasped, and nearly fell over backwards.

"Are these *words*?" she asked.

They were. Words in archaic text, floating in the glass.

"Ah...yes," Jezwe said. "Yes, but..."

"Can you read it?"

"Nearly."

He stared in silence for a time. There were symbols in use here that looked like errors, but which were probably the root symbols from which the archaic *he* knew evolved.

"All right," he said. "Over here...? This word is a greeting. 'Hello', or 'welcome'. Not sure what *this* part is. Gods, I wish Dungau were here."

"He's not," she said. "Keep going."

"*This* word...this is our home. In archaic. Before it, I think that means, um... 'fresh'. Or 'new.' And these little words, that's a determiner and a possessive?"

"I remember why I hate reading," she said. "What is the last word?"

"'List,' I think. Or 'contents.' It's not either of those, but nearly."

"So. Hello, something, something, fresh, Ter, something close to contents," she said. "That means nothing."

"'Earth.'"

"What?"

"*Ter* in archaic is called 'Earth,'" he said.

"Fine. That helps not at all. What does it *mean?*"

He chased synonyms around in his head for a bit, before coming up with something that almost worked. "Welcome, to, the, new, Earth...contents. I guess."

"New Earth contents," she repeated.

"I think so."

"What are these new contents?"

"I honestly don't know, Yyamo. Maybe you should touch it again, and we'll try this with different words."

She shrugged, and jabbed the barely comprehensible

sentence with a finger.

The glass changed again: neat rows of words filled up the entire panel.

"Excellent," Yyamo said. "More words, as requested. Any idea what *this* is?"

"Yes," Jezwe said, his eyes darting from one familiar word to the next, all across the glass. "It's food."

He chose a word he recognized as 'chicken' and touched it. The words floated away, and the glass panel began to hum.

"What's happening?" Yyamo asked.

"I think we've found the kitchen you were looking for," Jezwe said.

———

THE DISCOVERY of a source of food—beyond raw fish or dried beef—turned the search for the gods of the moon into a somewhat more leisurely exercise. The meals produced by the machinery were incredibly varied, and very good; so good, Jezwe thought less of returning home, and more of bringing others to the city, to share in the bounty.

After a lengthy search through dozens of closets, they found clothing for themselves. It was undeniably *odd* clothing—the gods preferred bright colors, and unnecessary snaps, zips, and fasteners—but a great improvement on the skin-tight diving underlayer.

They learned how it was that the grounds looked so well-tended, despite there being no gods around to do the tending: free-roaming machines did it. They also cleaned the floors—Yyamo had gotten in the habit of dropping food on the floor, just to watch a tiny box-on-wheels dart out from a hidden wall recess and retrieve it—and controlled the airflow, lighting, and heat.

The city ran entirely on its own.

Jezwe no longer expected to die at any moment. But he remained unsettled, as there remained bigger mysteries to solve.

Then, one night, Yyamo decided to go for a swim.

She woke Jezwe from a sound slumber in the housing unit he'd chosen for himself—it had a muted blue painting on the wall that didn't look like anything, which he nonetheless found compelling in a way he couldn't put in words—with an announcement over the city's loudspeaker system.

"Jezwe, wake up, I need you," she said.

Cursing himself for discovering the loudspeaker, and for showing it to Yyamo, he engaged the speaker in the room, and responded. "Why? What's the matter?"

"It's the fish," she said. "They're gone."

This was no exaggeration. He was at the pond a few minutes later; the water was clear, as always, and devoid of life.

"There's less water, as well," Yyamo said. "Look at the level."

"We did not consume *that* much water," Jezwe said. "Nor all the fish."

"I've eaten *no* fish. And hardly any water, once I learned the archaic for ale."

"Then who *is* consuming it?" he wondered.

"Do the *machines* eat?" she asked.

He thought back to the very first observation he made, the day the dragon spat them out: there should have been more fish.

"Machines don't eat," he said. "They cook, and they clean, and they throw things away. Yyamo, I have a terrible idea. I think it's time we went outside."

THEY'D ALREADY WORKED out how the machines disposed of waste. In Yyamo's quest to discover the "back of the barroom," she'd found the waste management area. All trash—from the dropped food in the dining area and the overripe fruit in the orchard, to the grass clippings from the coliseum and the human waste in the plumbing—was aggregated, in tubs, in the only unpleasant room in the entire city. Once collected, a machine would take it outside, through a double-sealed exit.

Out of the city, the mechanized garbage bin carrier transited across the surface, along a flat cobblestone path that curled behind a nearby building, and out of view. It returned an hour later, with an empty bin.

They had not been able to find an angle, in any part of the city, that revealed what was at the other end of the cobblestone path. Perhaps nobody wanted a view.

This should have been where the answer to the mystery died, except: in a small alcove, beside the double-sealed exit, there lived a deep water diving outfit. That was what Jezwe thought he was looking at, initially. The suit he wore while trapped inside the dragon's belly, and the suit in the waste management room, shared much in common.

But *this* one was for walking on the moon.

They had not used it; the need to understand where the trash ultimately ended up was not more powerful, at that time, than the fear of attempting a moonwalk.

It was now.

Yyamo worked out how to get the oxygen for the suit working in a few minutes; longer, to work out how to seal Jezwe inside of it. They decided it had to be him, mainly because it was a better fit, and additionally because it was his foolish idea to do this at all.

"I remain insufficiently invested in the mystery to go out *there* in order to resolve it," Yyamo said.

THERE WASN'T much of a learning curve when it came to walking on the surface. Jezwe already spent a day in a similar suit, and close to a month now in the moon's gravity—which he did not expect to differ, whether he was standing inside or outside the city.

Where the learning curve was steepest, was in figuring out how to work the double-sealed exit. This involved reading a lot of archaic text, arguing with the machine, and some cursing, but they eventually got him through, without also exposing Yyamo.

The greatest risk Jezwe faced, once outside, was in trying to move too quickly. He wanted to *solve* this, finally, and the answer was just ahead and around the corner, but—and this *felt* true but was probably not—thought it certain that should he jump *too* high, with no ceiling to contain him, he'd just continue upwards, off the moon, and toward the same fate he'd expected while inside the dragon.

So, he took his time.

The path continued around the corner and straight off, away from the city. Sunlight lit the way forward.

He kept going, until he reached the crater.

It seemed the city of the moon gods had been built next to a canyon-like crater, and the machines were using it as a dump.

He stepped to the edge—slowly, very, very slowly—and looked down.

The first thing to notice was the fish: hundreds of thousands of them—far more than he and Yyamo arrived with—dead and uncorrupted, in a tall, neat mound. Traveling a little further around the lip, he reached a different pile: cows. Again, hundreds, if not thousands of them; dead, from exposure to the surface, but uncorrupted, either because rot needed air, or because the gods decided upon a very peculiar miracle.

There were more towers of protein to come: pigs, chickens, goats, deer, and an assortment of other four-legged beasts for which he had no name. Then came the produce, and the grains, and beans, and plants he didn't recognize. All told, there was enough food in the crater to feed the planet from which it was harvested for a generation.

There was more, at the bottom of the far end. The crater was deep enough that most of the floor was in shadows despite the sun overhead, but there was something high enough over there to capture light, and shiny enough to reflect it.

Jezwe kept going.

Halfway around, he discovered a downhill walkway carved into the side of the crater, that terminated at a point below the sunlight. He traveled down that far, and then—when the light began to fail—some mechanism within his suit engaged, and a light source atop the helmet made itself known.

He continued, until reaching an artificial platform. He tilted the helmet downward from there, to bathe the floor in light, and gasped.

Bodies.

Not animals this time, but people. People dressed in garish, brightly colored clothing with too many snaps, zips, and fasteners, piled unceremoniously in a heap on the crater's floor.

He hurried down to get a better look, no longer concerned that in moving too rapidly he might unintentionally gain orbit. This was unwise; in his haste, he tripped and fell right over the side of the walkway... fortunately, not far. The pile of corpses met him well before he hit bottom.

Abruptly face-to-face with the twisted, half rotted face of a woman no older than Yyamo, Jezwe screamed, and panicked, two things that were not recommended in this circumstance.

He scrambled back across more corpses—old and young and in-between—trying to run and climb and crawl out of the mass grave as quickly as he could.

He arrived—eventually—back at the walkway, albeit at a

lower point than where he left it. Then he sat for a time, to regain his breath and his senses.

These bodies weren't like that of the fish, or the cows, or the pigs; they were partly decomposed, and if the boils and rashes and sores on their heads and arms were any indication, what killed them was *not* exposure, but some sort of disease.

They died in their beds, he realized. *And the machines dumped them here, as it does with all the trash.*

"I have found our gods, father," he said. "I have found them, and they are dead. Who shall we pray to now?"

***

"I THINK I would like to be a weather god," Yyamo said, one night.

This was some two dozen days after Jezwe discovered the crater. He knew this because the sun had recently set, and imagined it coincided with the phases of the moon. They had no other means with which to tell time, not until one of them became proficient enough to get a machine to do it.

"Does it matter?" Jezwe asked. "What kind of god you are."

They were lying on the floor, beneath the great crystal dome in the grand pavilion. It was the best place to look at the stars, and the planet they used to call home.

"I suppose not," she said. "But I like the idea of someone praying to me for rain, or for no *more* rain, or whatever other weather-related inconvenience they are looking to amend. And I will do nothing for them."

"Because you can't control the weather."

"Just as it is with *all* moon gods."

They felt a rumble.

"Here it comes," Yyamo said.

The latest dragon to leave its nest rocketed away. It would

collect more of what the moon no longer needed—cattle, fish, wheat—to be dumped in the crater with the rest of it. The city's last residents—before dying—failed to tell the machines to stop pillaging the planet below, and Jezwe couldn't figure out how to do it either, so all he could do was watch.

"I wonder if they've noticed us," Jezwe said.

"On Ter? I hope so. I am looking forward to being worshiped." Yyamo got to her feet. "Anyway. Let's have a look at that library you found. Time I learned to read."

"Yes," he said. "We should do that. In a minute."

She looked at him with a trace of concern. That his melancholy remained, despite their remarkable good fortune, continued to frustrate Yyamo. Jezwe knew this, but couldn't do much about it. "Not *too* long," she said. "No rest for lesser moon gods."

"I'll be there soon."

Yyamo left, and he was alone with his thoughts, and the slowly rotating planet Ter.

It would be winter soon in the Great Lake region. He wondered if this was something he could see with the naked eye. He had no other means, because the city of the moon gods had no great observatorium, no massive lunascope. They were *people*, these gods; they would have needed magnifying lenses to see across great distances. And yet, he'd looked everywhere, and found nothing.

As we see, so are we seen. This was the principle on which their faith was grounded. But even when the gods were *alive*, there was no one looking back. The gods may have been *seen* at one time, but they never *saw*. They never even cared to look.

"See me, Dongau," he said. "See me and listen. For I have doubt."

HYPNOPOMPIC CIRCUMSTANCE

Thomas's first encounter with the alien was terrifying.

It happened in his bedroom. Thom was attempting to get to sleep at the time, after a long Friday night that had extended into early Saturday morning. Alcohol was involved, and a little pot, but nothing natively hallucinogenic, not unless someone slipped him something. Nothing that could explain the appearance of someone who wasn't supposed to be there.

Thom was still in his clothes—undressing being too much work—with the bass beat of the last song he heard running a tight circuit around his skull. It refused to leave, because Thomas didn't know the rest of the song. He decided it would either go away with sleep, or it would be in his head forever. There were no other options. Likewise, for the taste of vodka and tonic with a splash of bile that convinced him it was time to stop drinking and time to start finding a way home. It would either be gone in the morning, or this was for the rest of his life.

The connective tissue between his thoughts began to fray. He was going over one particular conversation with Carl about patently dishonest distressed property reselling tactics which Carl swore by, and then another conversation intervened in which Ned declared Tina a bitch, and then Tina was there screaming about an open house and the bass beat on *what the hell is the name of that song* kicked in again and it all made sense to Thomas that the song lied about the bathtub, *Tina*, and Carl doesn't care about the siding so let's all here comes the *chorus* and SOMEONE WAS IN THE ROOM.

Thomas was lying on his back. Not two minutes earlier, his body was fully capable of moving about the apartment, but now it wasn't at all up to the task. He could open his eyes—which he did, as soon as he sensed he wasn't alone—but that was all. He was completely paralyzed.

The alien was super tall. Six foot five, at least. It was thin and all angles, like a piece of ambulatory scaffolding, with a long cloak and a hood. It had a head shaped like an upside-down teardrop, and eyes that took up half of its face.

Thomas couldn't make out anything else about the alien, or turn his head to see the rest of the room. (Was he the *only* alien there? It could be a whole team.) It was too dark, and he couldn't move to reach the light, the floor, or the baseball bat in the corner. The pillow under his head might do as a weapon, perhaps, but again: he couldn't move. He couldn't even scream out loud.

The alien reached out with a gray-skinned hand that had only three fingers and a thumb—the fingers were unaccountably long and had an extra knuckle—to touch the side of Thomas's face.

Thomas gave screaming another try. It still didn't work, but his heart, which was now beating four times faster than the bass beat still stuck in his head, might have been audible by then.

And then, thankfully, Thom passed out.

THOMAS WOKE up still in his own bed Saturday morning, still in his clothes. His room looked just like it had when he passed out the night before. Everything looked normal, *so* normal that he didn't even remember the alien until he got out of bed, and then only after a lengthy internal conversation:

Oh good, I can move.

Wait, why was I worried about this?

Was there a chance I wouldn't be able to move?

Yes, I remember not being able to move.

When was that?

...

When the ALIEN WAS IN THE BEDROOM.

In the frantic moments that followed, Thomas removed all of his clothes and checked every body part he could get in front of the bathroom mirror for evidence of obvious physical trauma or general malfeasance. He came away from this review deciding that he needed to get back into the gym, but otherwise satisfied that the alien hadn't *obviously* poked or probed him.

The next thing he did was verify that it was indeed Saturday, and also that it was the *correct* Saturday. He wasn't missing any time, not counting the time he slept. If he'd been abducted (of course he wasn't abducted) it was a very brief abduction.

Satisfied and already naked, he decided to bathe.

By the time Thomas was showered and shaved, dressed and holding a cup of coffee in his hands, he'd convinced himself that the thing which seemed utterly and totally true—that there was an alien in his bedroom—had actually been conjured by his imagination. Yes, it was correct that he'd ingested no hallucinogens (knowingly) and yes, nothing like this had ever happened to him before. Also yes, in the past his senses had always proven to be dependable in arraigning the external world and his mind had always been good about evaluating what the senses reported in a way that conformed with basic reality. Even when he was drunk and/or stoned. There was no reason to think that had changed.

Ergo, it never happened.

That was the only reasonable conclusion. It never happened, so he could go on with his day, and his life without worrying that a six foot five gray-skinned bulbous-headed alien with three fingers and extra knuckles had a key to his apartment and was maybe, possibly, doing things to him while he slept.

It was ridiculous to think otherwise.

THEN IT HAPPENED AGAIN. Sort of.

Thomas was in the business of selling real estate, which was why he had to work on a Saturday. It was also why he'd spent all of Friday night drinking with Carl, Ned, Indira, Louis, Ciera and Doug: because he didn't *like* selling real estate.

He also wasn't great at it. An argument could be made that Thomas might enjoy it if he was better at it, but he was pretty sure it only worked the other way around, i.e., he would only be good at it if he liked it.

There was a third argument, which was that it was possible to be good at selling real estate while also hating real estate, provided one sufficiently liked making money. This was Carl's approach, and it was great insofar as it justified all sorts of dishonest strategies because they accomplished the goal of making money.

The property he was trying to sell on Saturday was a vacation home belonging to a neurologist named Alek. It was a gorgeous place overlooking a lake, practically designed to make anyone who couldn't afford it hate their own lives. It was *so* nice that when/if it sold, Thomas's commission would be sufficient to live off of without selling another property for about eight months.

This only made him hate it more.

(That he even *had* the listing was something of a miracle. Alek, for whatever reason, seemed to like Thomas and think him competent at his job, which he really wasn't.)

It was a lousy way to spend a Saturday. About twenty-five people showed up for the open house, and the two or three who could afford it—if their default public persona is rude and dismissive, they can afford it—didn't look truly interested. Thom had to hold a fake smile and an engaging tone for about two hours longer than any man should have been expected to, while despising the fact that he was there at all, and when it was done he had nothing to show for it other than a sore face from all the smiling.

He skipped the bar in favor of a quick sandwich, and an early bed, choosing, *end the bad day as soon as possible,* over, *try drinking until the day improves.*

No alien showed up as he drifted off. This would have been cause for celebration—it had indeed been a hallucination, perhaps triggered by too much of something—but he was asleep and couldn't celebrate. Nor could he do so the following morning because that was when the alien *did* appear.

Thomas had been in that half-awake state where the dream he was having—he didn't solidly recall what it had been about, but he did remember being somewhere public and missing his pants—when he got that same weird sensation that there was someone else in the room.

When he opened his eyes, he saw he was facing the left side of his bed. Generally, the view of that part of the room consisted of a nightstand with a book he'd been meaning to get back to, a lamp, an alarm clock, a chair being used to hold clothing, and a window. On this morning, all the other stuff was there, but now an alien was sitting in the chair.

Thomas tried screaming, but as before he couldn't seem to move.

"Do you like your life?" the alien asked. It had a tiny mouth at the bottom of that bulbous face that seemed too small to produce real sound. "I'm just curious. You don't seem happy."

Thom slammed his eyes shut.

Not real, not real, it's not real, he thought. Then he felt something touch his cheek.

He screamed again—this time out loud—and sat up in bed, recoiling from the contact.

There was nobody in the room. The clothes on the chair were right where they were supposed to be, and the alien was exactly as nonexistent as *it* was supposed to be.

Once Thomas got his heart to stop pounding, he lay back down on the pillow, closed his eyes most of the way and looked at that side of the room again. The chair was holding his dark blue suit. It was *possible* that the suit plus the shadows from the curtain over the window conspired to *look* like an alien, especially since Thomas was already predisposed to look for one in his bedroom.

Yes, he decided, *that's all it is.* Then he stopped putting his clothes on the chair.

ONLY, it kept happening. A couple of times a week, either just before he fell asleep or just before he woke up, the alien would appear, talk to him for a few seconds or not, and then disappear back into the dark recesses of Thomas's evidently overtaxed imagination.

Thom tried not sleeping, but that didn't end up being a

viable option. He borrowed some sleeping pills from Ciera—he claimed not being able to move Alek's property was keeping him up nights—to see if *sleeping too much* worked better than *not sleeping enough*, but it didn't.

Weirdly, he was starting to get used to it. Sure, he was always paralyzed and the alien was innately disturbing, but it hadn't *done* anything to him. It mostly just sat there. It was still terrifying, but no longer *I am falling to my death* terrifying. More like, *I was nearly hit by a car*: a sudden shock, and then relief at still being alive.

And the alien asked the *strangest* questions.

"How was your day?"

"Do you enjoy this weather?"

"What do you want to do with your life? Is it this? Or something else?"

"Do you have a favorite color? Does everyone? Mine is ultraviolet."

"Why do you care so much about what other people think of you?"

"You seem anxious. Do you like what you do for work?"

One morning, he didn't ask any questions at all. He just said, "I'm being rude. My name is Gerald." Then he left.

What was a little interesting was that as the questions continued ("Does everyone work all their lives like this?" "Are you dating someone?") Thomas began asking himself the same questions. Because some of what Gerald wanted to know was sort of dumb—Thomas couldn't speak for everyone, but he didn't personally *have* a favorite color—but for most questions, even if Thomas *had* the power to respond he didn't know what he'd say.

Despite being used to Gerald, then, Thomas still wasn't getting a lot of sleep. Not because Gerald was a manifested figment of Thom's imagination, given form in order to torture him. It was that the nature of the torture was in forcing Thomas into questioning everything he was doing with his life.

One day—finally—Thomas confided in someone about the alien. This was less a decision on Thomas's part and more of a thing being blurted out of his mouth without him being a party to it. Certainly, his *choice* of confidantes was poor: his client, Alek. Probably, the last thing the man wanted to know was that his realtor was actively hallucinating.

He and Thom were in the middle of a strategy meeting at Alek's primary residence in the city, a condo in a style that everyone at the office called *upscale drug lord*. Alek had just finished saying something requiring a response from Thomas, but Thomas hadn't registered this in any way. He'd drifted back to the prior evening, when the alien asked why Thomas drank so much.

"Thom?" Alek said. "You there?"

"Yes, sorry. Sorry. What were you saying?"

Alek shook his head and headed to the coffee maker. They were in his kitchen for this meeting.

"You seem distracted, if you don't mind my saying," Alek said. He handed Thom a cup of black coffee. "Everything all right at home?"

"Yes, everything's...neurologist, right?"

"That's what my degree says, sure," Alek said. "Are you looking for one?"

"And that's, nerves. Neural pathways. The brain."

Alek smiled. "Thom, I was joking. If you have a medical problem, you should really talk to your own doctor."

"Yeah, I don't know what I have."

"All right." Alek checked his watch, and then pulled up a stool. "What are the symptoms?"

"Aliens," Thom said.

It just fell out of his mouth. Later, he'd come to understand how desperately he needed to talk to someone about this but in the moment, he was mostly just horrified.

"I mean, *an* alien," he clarified. "It keeps showing up in my bedroom. I know it isn't real, but knowing that doesn't stop it from showing up. I don't know what to do, but...I thought maybe there might be something wrong with my head."

To his immense credit, Alek neither laughed nor fired Thomas on the spot.

"Have you tried asking the alien what it wants?" he asked.

"I can't. When he shows up I can't move at all, except my eyes."

"I see," Alek said. "Well, I'm the wrong kind of head doctor for that."

"I know, I know. But I thought maybe you'd encountered something like this before."

"Not personally."

Alek pondered over his coffee cup for a few seconds, while Thomas enumerated the many reasons talking about this to a client was a bad idea.

"Alien, huh," Alek said. "*Specifically* an alien."

"I don't know what else to call it."

"All right look, here's some free advice. Go online and check out hypnopompic hallucinations. Or hypnogogic. One's when you're falling asleep and one's when you're waking up; I forget which is which."

"Hallucinations."

"Yeah, man, it's either that or a real space alien is visiting you. If that's what you think, you're *definitely* talking to the wrong person. It's just your body waking up in the wrong order and your brain not knowing its awake at all. With sleep paralysis thrown in, your head can end up in all kinds of unusual places."

Thom decided not to ask what sleep paralysis was. Alek

assumed he knew, and he was already feeling self-conscious about having brought this up.

"The point is," Alek said, "not only is it not real, it's not all that unusual. You woke up halfway, freaked out because you couldn't move, and your imagination filled in an alien. If you were more of a religious type you could've seen an angel or a devil instead. A few hundred years back it probably would have been a succubus. So relax."

"Wow," Thomas said, "that's a huge relief, thanks."

"You're welcome. But do me a favor and talk to a psychiatrist anyway."

"I'll find one." Thomas laughed. "Probably just ask me the same questions the alien's been asking."

Alek was supposed to laugh at that. He didn't, and Thomas felt awkward all over again.

"Yeah, hypnopompic hallucinations don't usually talk. Is it... telling you to do stuff?"

"It usually just asks about my day."

Alek stared at him for an uncomfortably long beat.

Now I've said too much, Thomas thought.

"Anyway," Thom said. "You're right, I'm sure it's nothing."

"Yeah of course," Alek said. "But definitely speak to someone, man. I can get you some names. Until then, keep in mind it's all in your head."

TINA REASSIGNED Alek's listing a week later—to Carl, of course. Thom considered asking Alek for an explanation, but he was pretty sure he wasn't going to like any of the possible answers. It was true that Thomas hadn't been able to sell the vacation house within the anticipated timeframe, but it was also true that Thom had confessed to visual and auditory hallucinations. The second thing was probably a bigger problem.

I'd have fired me too, he thought.

Over the course of that same week, Thom had looked up the definitions of hypnopompic hallucination, sleep paralysis, and auditory hallucination. The word *schizophrenia* came up a lot. He didn't *think* he was schizophrenic, but that was probably not an easy thing to self-diagnose.

Meanwhile, Thom's work was suffering. He began to worry that Alek hadn't just asked for a new realtor—he'd *told* Tina about the alien. Other listings started to get pulled from under him, and drinks after work stopped being quite so common. In fact, they were rare enough that he began to wonder if they were just meeting at a different bar without him.

He would have straight-up asked one of them about it but since *paranoia* was one of the symptoms the internet said he should be on the lookout for, he actively overcompensated in the opposite direction.

He also didn't speak to a psychiatrist. He did pick one to call, and even went so far as to plug the number into his phone, but he couldn't bring himself to connect the call.

Meanwhile, Gerald the alien stubbornly refused to stop showing up, despite not existing. He continued to drop in two or three times a week, always with a new question or a variation of an old one. It was like a recurring nightmare, where Thomas was trapped in the middle of a personality survey with no way to respond. Only, he wasn't sleeping so it couldn't be a nightmare.

ONE MORNING, Gerald asked if Thom was having trouble at work.

"I ask because you're not sleeping well," the alien noted.

Gerald lacked the basic awareness necessary to work out that *he* was the problem, and not the rest of Thomas's life. Thom didn't have a *great* life before the alien visitations began, but it wasn't *terrible*. And yes, at the time the question was posed he *was* having trouble at work. Tina had just suggested he take some time off, which wasn't really a thing in a commission-based industry and she knew it. He told her he was fine, maybe a little too loudly, because Doug and Louis were in her office barely a second later, to calmly suggest he call it a day.

So he did. He left. He did *not* slam the door on his way out; he just closed it more forcefully than he meant to. It didn't break or anything. Then he went to the bar, alone, and drank until the sun went down, and he went to bed, and woke up to Gerald the chatty alien wanting to know how Thom's job was going and if he was getting enough rest.

YOU AREN'T REAL, Thom screamed. *GO AWAY BECAUSE YOU AREN'T REAL AND I CAN'T TAKE THIS ANYMORE.*

He couldn't *actually* scream it; he thought it loudly.

Amazingly, Gerald acted like it *had* been spoken aloud. He...recoiled. He had a nearly expressionless face, and yet he managed to look wounded.

And then hew was gone, and Thomas could move.

Thom spent the entire day—a day in which he hosted an open house for a distressed property where the most valuable thing in the place was the donuts he brought—wondering if this had done it, and he'd finally banished the alien from his unconscious mind.

He had not. Gerald returned that night.

Thom *greatly* preferred the morning visitations to the evening ones. Nighttime appearances were more frightening for some reason, even if Gerald didn't really look much different regardless of the time. The alien seemed to be aware of this, as he mostly showed up in the morning. He also didn't usually drop in back-to-back.

On this night, Gerald did something new. Rather than ask probing questions, he picked up the long-neglected book from Thom's nightstand, flipped past the page Thomas had left off, and began reading.

Thomas fell asleep after about five sentences.

The following morning, as soon as he was awake Thomas flipped open the book to the bookmarked page. It was *not* where Thomas had left off; the bookmark was now three-quarters of the way through. Nothing on the page looked like anything Thomas had previously read. But he did find what Gerald had read out loud. All five sentences. And he'd read it word-for-word.

He's real, Thom realized. *And I know how to talk to him now.*

But he still couldn't, because Gerald didn't reappear that night, or the next night, or the night after that.

And then a week passed, and Thomas decided he must have finally done it. He'd gotten rid of his alien.

This didn't positively impact his overall mood; if anything, it made his general demeanor worse.

Instead of worrying that Gerald might show, he spent his nights awake and going over the alien's questions, again and again.

Thomas was *not* happy. He did *not* like his job. He didn't like his friends, he hadn't been in a serious relationship for three years, and he was doing *nothing* with his life.

What he was instead, was angry all the time.

Thomas didn't have anyone he could talk to about any of it. But he *used* to. He could talk to Gerald, if only Gerald would come back again.

After another week passed, Thomas took to leaving apologetic notes for Gerald on the bedside table, and talking to his ceiling.

"I'm sorry if I offended you," he said. "Please come back."

But every night, Thom fell asleep alone and every morning, woke up alone.

THE MONTH that followed was a bad one for Thomas.

It began okay. His work friends seemed to have concluded that Thom was *back to normal*, so he was getting invited to go out again, which was...okay. It didn't bring him much joy, and the longer he spent with them the more he realized they weren't friends at all; they were just coworkers. The only thing they all had in common was selling property *for* people they loudly despised *to* people they loudly despised.

He begrudged them for the word *normal,* too. He didn't know what they thought his personal normal was, but didn't think he'd behaved any different, outwardly, before, during or after Gerald came into his life. He had maybe been a little short with a couple of them, but he wasn't getting a lot of sleep at the time; real friends would understand that.

Inwardly? If *normal* was to be interpreted as *before an extraterrestrial proved its existence to him*, Thomas didn't think he'd ever get back to that.

Still, he tried going through the motions of his prior existence. But his ability to sell property to or for anybody had, if anything, gotten worse. Whereas when Gerald was around, Thomas zombie-talked his way through his appointments—which was bad enough—now that the alien was gone Thomas had begun self-sabotaging.

He couldn't help himself. When showing a property,

instead of skipping past the flaws—and he always knew where the flaws were in his listings—he kept bringing prospective buyers *right to* them.

Whatever hope Thomas had that he'd be getting over this eventually and going back to living his life—and again, to *normal*—fell apart the night after Alek's vacation home finally sold.

It took Carl nearly as long to sell it as it took Thomas to *not* sell it, because the neurosurgeon was asking for too much and seemed content to wait until someone came along willing to pay too much. To that end, Carl was actually a better match, because what he did—and what Thomas was unwilling to do— was lie, outrageously, about the neighbors. This was his favorite trick. Taking Carl at his word, nearly every property in town was just around the corner from the family of a famous actor, sports figure, or pop singer.

The occasion of the sale called for a trip to the bar. Everyone got loud drunk. And Carl got to be Carl.

"To Thomas," he said, some untold number of drinks into the evening, "for sucking so bad."

Carl laughed. Nobody else did, not until Thom smiled, albeit thinly, to let them know it was okay.

"I'm kidding, I'm kidding," Carl said. "Look, I feel bad. Tell you what, I'll split the commission. You can have..." He acted like he was doing the math. "Five percent. What do you say?"

Thomas was pretty sure Tina had told Carl to split the commission already, and this was a performance. That just made it more grating.

"It's okay," Thomas said. "I don't want your five percent."

"Aw come on," Carl said.

"I think that's really nice," Ciera said.

Doug, who only six weeks earlier was partly responsible for

escorting Thomas from Tina's office, clapped him on the shoulders and said, "yeah, that's really generous."

Thom looked into the faces of the people around him and saw nothing he liked.

"No thanks," he said, standing, "I'm not interested in your pity."

He turned to walk away from the table when he heard Carl say, "why don't you ask the alien?"

Thomas lost his temper then.

Really lost it.

He couldn't say how he ended up on the other side of the table, only that he *did*, and once he was there he had Carl's collar in one hand while he was punching Carl in the face with the other hand.

He was told later—by the police officer in charge of escorting him from the bar to a jail cell—that it took four people to pull him off of Carl.

He had no memory of this.

Thomas was released on his own recognizance the next morning, once he proved sober and lucid. Carl—who got a nice ride from the bar to the hospital—didn't press charges, but that was the *only* positive to come out it.

Two days later, Tina notified Thomas that he would no longer be affiliated with her real estate firm, and that was that. He was effectively out of a job.

Another five days passed, in which Thomas did nothing but sit in his apartment, ice his swollen fist, and sleep. He talked to Gerald quite a lot during that time, but got no response.

On day six, he agreed to go into the office the following morning to fill out paperwork and clear his desk. This would no doubt be conducted in front of armed security or something. Which was stupid: Thomas wasn't a threat. Carl was just an asshole. He thought everyone could agree to that. Even Carl.

Lying in bed that night, staring at the ceiling and waiting for sleep and/or Gerald to arrive, Thom wondered what he was going to do with his life now that he'd burned down what little he had so far.

Then he wondered if he wanted to live at all.

WHEN HE OPENED his eyes the next morning he couldn't move, which was fantastic news.

Gerald was there again, standing beside the bed, all six feet and five inches of him looming over Thomas.

Thomas tried to think-scream an apology, but he didn't have a chance.

"Don't go to the office today," Gerald said.

Then he was gone, and Thomas could move again.

"Why not?" he asked the ceiling. "*Why not*, Gerald? Come back here and tell me why not!"

He stumbled out of bed and for some reason decided to search the house, as if after all this time the alien hadn't been appearing out of nothing at all; he was just hiding in the linen closet.

Of *course* Gerald wasn't in the linen closet or any of the other closets, or the shower, under the bed or behind the couch. Thom looked anyway, not yet prepared to admit that his alien friend reappeared specifically and only to say something cryptic before vanishing.

Defeated, Thomas cycled through a shower and a shave, Gerald's words echoing in his head like that bass beat from the first night.

Don't go to the office today.

He'd already decided what clothes to wear while being formally escorted from the premises. Something casual but not *too* casual. An *I am cool with not being here anymore* look that said he was a guy on his way up, rather than who he was, which was someone who'd just as soon set his real estate license on fire.

He knew they were talking about him and wanted them to understand that he didn't care.

Why do you care so much about what other people think of you?

Thomas decided he *cared* that they were left with the impression that he *didn't* care. He had no reason to; he'd never be working with any of them again, never *see* any of them again if he had his way. And the odds were pretty good that most of them wouldn't even be in the office, not unless they decided, collectively, to attend the formal drumming-out.

He could wear the khakis, loafers, and button-down shirt, act like he was heading to his yacht after this unsavory business was resolved, and it would make no difference. He could show up in a bathrobe, blue jeans and sandals and it would also make no difference.

In that context, the idea of simply not showing up at all didn't come off as unreasonable.

I'm sorry, something came up, he could say. *Something in my important and busy life that took precedence over returning to the office for such trifles. Maybe we can do this next week?*

Do you like what you do?

It was strange, but Gerald's suggestion that he *not* go into the office on this day had somehow given Thomas a sense of agency over his life—however temporary—that he didn't have before. He was always where other people told him to be, when they told him to be there, whether it was Tina at the office, his clients, or the team heading to the bar. Stupidly, this one potentially rebellious act—of *not* going in when he said he would—felt like an act of liberation.

Liberation was a low hurdle. Especially when the only

reason he was thinking about it at all was because someone *else* told him to stay home. Sure, that someone else was a space alien who may actually be evidence of a psychotic break, but he was still doing something someone else told him to do.

Unfortunately, going into the office was a binary problem. Tina told him to go, and Gerald told him not to, and there was no third option. He couldn't defy *both* of them so his only *real* agency was deciding which one to ignore.

His act of performative defiance would have to take place at some other time.

The trip down this deterministic rabbit hole took up half of Thomas's morning somehow, and soon it was well past time for him to have left in order to make it to the office as scheduled, especially if he intended to exit the apartment in clothing. In this way, he managed to make a decision by failing to make any decisions.

Close enough, he thought. He put on his bathrobe, turned on the living room television, and went about finding something to eat.

An hour later, he decided it would be best if he let Tina know that due to a difficult-to-describe decision-point paralysis he would not be leaving the apartment today. (He would find a better way to phrase that.) So he called the office.

It went straight to voicemail, directing him to press zero to hear the directory listing the other available realtors, given Tina's current unavailability. He pressed zero and listened to all the names, noting as he did so that *his* name was no longer an option.

He tried Ciera next, and got the same message about pressing zero. Same with Indira, and Doug, Louis and Ned. Not even Carl was picking up.

Thomas's paranoia spoke up to suggest that they were all perhaps avoiding him, but that was ridiculous; he was expected there a half an hour ago. If anything, they should have been eager to hear from him.

That was when he noticed the chyron on the bottom of the television screen. He'd been watching an episode of a serialized fantasy series about which he knew nothing (it had magic and vampires and looked sort of cool) but now there was a bulletin at the bottom, which read, DOWNTOWN EXPLOSION ROCKS CITY. A few seconds later, a local news anchor was apologizing for interrupting the regular programming, but the "possible gas main eruption" that destroyed two blocks of businesses downtown was too important to wait for the *News At Noon*.

The anchor read off the location, while at the same time a camera shot from a drone over the city confirmed the same thing visually: the real estate office was right in the middle of the blast.

THE POLICE WERE at Thomas's door a week later.

He'd spent most of that week in his bathrobe, with the clothes he would have died in still draped on the chair in his bedroom. Both times he left the house was for food, and only after giving Gerald plenty of opportunity to notify him *not* to, if he were so inclined.

He was not. Once again, the alien didn't show, which was terrible. Thomas would have been in the office when the main exploded were it not for Gerald, and now Thom was afraid to do anything at all. His new way of taking charge of his own life was to say *no* when the world said, *you should really leave the apartment.*

The local news's ongoing forensics of the downtown explosion was utterly engrossing. The death count was up to forty-nine, with over two hundred injuries. Tina was one of the forty-nine and so was Doug, and Louis, and Ciera. Indira wasn't, nor Ned or Carl. So far. They were still adding to the list.

Thomas wasn't being counted among the dead either. Nobody had called or come by for a wellness check and it wasn't a secret that he was *supposed* to be there at around the time the explosion happened, and he hadn't *told* anyone that he was still alive, but they hadn't declared him dead anyway.

This led to Thomas being unduly preoccupied with the mechanism involved in developing an accurate headcount. The real estate office was at the epicenter of the explosion so there were no bodies to recover, which probably meant the only way to get included among the dead was to have someone report you missing. Self-evidently, there was nobody in Thomas's life who could do that. (Aside from Gerald, who they probably wouldn't believe.) This meant, perversely, that if Thomas *was* in the office at that time, he *still* wouldn't be counted among the dead.

For about an hour, Thomas took seriously the notion that he *had* gone down there and *was* currently dead.

He resolved this by ordering a pizza.

Because of his new asceticism, when the police arrived at the door they didn't get to meet the young, successful, definitely-going-places version of Thomas he had intended to convey by wearing the clothes draped on the chair. They got to meet someone who hadn't shaved in seven days or showered in three, and hadn't held a proper conversation with another human being in about two weeks.

It was not a good first impression.

The lead detective introduced himself, asked if Thomas was indeed Thomas, and then asked if he and the two uniformed officers waiting in the hall could all please come inside to have a conversation.

"I wasn't expecting anyone," Thomas said, as if this wasn't

obvious. Aside from the facial hair and—presumably, although he couldn't smell it himself—three days of funk, he was in a bathrobe and boxers, with no shirt.

"We're not looking for a dinner party," the detective said. "We just need to ask you a few questions."

His name was Naughton. He had a disarming smile.

"Sure, come on in," Thom said.

Naughton took a look at the couch, and the pizza boxes on the floor next to the couch, and opted for the folding chair in the corner instead. (The couch was the only thing Thom had in the living room to sit upon. The folding chair was there if he ever had more than two people over, which had not yet happened.)

"Is this about the explosion?" Thom asked, sitting in his usual spot on the couch. He realized the television was still on, so he clicked it off with the remote, to be polite.

"It is, yes," Naughton said. "I understand you were supposed to be downtown that day. Is that right?"

"I was, but I decided not to go. Lucky me, right?"

"Very lucky. Very lucky. You were meeting with Mrs. Wainscot, is that right?"

"Tina, yeah. I was clearing out. But, you know, I figured I could do that another day."

"You changed your mind."

"Yes."

"Right. Okay" He flipped to another page in his notes. Naughton was working off a small pad of paper. It seemed inefficient, but Thomas didn't think it was his place to say so.

"You were also involved in an incident about a week earlier, is that right? A Mr. Fellowes was hospitalized? Carl Fellowes?"

"That was...yes. Yes, that's true, but what does that have to do with the explosion? Did Carl say something?"

Naughton didn't answer that.

"According to the report, you assaulted Mr. Fellowes, which

is what led to Mrs. Wainscot's decision to sever, is that essentially correct?"

"He wasn't in the hospital," Thomas said. "Carl. He wasn't in the hospital. They checked him out and he went home. Didn't stay overnight."

"Must've really pissed you off," the detective said, smiling.

"Sure, I guess."

He closed his notepad.

"Look, Thom—can I call you Thom?"

"Sure."

"Thom, this is just a loose end, do you understand?"

"Not really, no."

"A loose end. You punch your friend Carl in the face—"

"Carl isn't my friend."

"All right. You punch your business associate Carl in the face because he made you angry. You lose your job. Boss asks you to come in and clear out your desk. You *don't* go in, and boom. The whole block goes up. You see where I'm going?"

"Not at all."

He grumbled and looked at his notes again.

"Why don't you tell me why you weren't there that day?" he asked.

"I told you, I decided not to go."

"But *why* did you decide not to go? I mean, that's pretty lucky, right? A little more luck than makes sense from where I'm sitting."

It'd been a long time since Thom had interacted with another human being. It wasn't as fun as he remembered.

"It was an accident," Thom said.

"You weren't there by accident?"

"The gas main. What does it matter why I wasn't there if it was an accident?"

Naughton looked at one of the uniformed cops with a comically exaggerated *what is he talking about?* expression. The cop shrugged.

Thom didn't know where the other cop had gone.

Is my apartment being searched right now? he wondered.

"Who told you it was an accident?" Naughton asked.

Thom pointed at the television. "Everyone," he said. "That's what they're saying on the news."

"Sure, they're saying that *now*. The thing about a blast this big, it's really hard to pinpoint whether something happened just *because*, or if someone meant for it to happen."

"Like terrorists?"

"Sure, like terrorists. Except they like to brag about this kinda thing and we haven't heard anybody doing that. Look, Thom, just tell me what made you decide not to go in that day, I'll write it down in my notebook here, and we'll be on our way. You can go back to...whatever you've got going on here."

"It was a friend, that's all. A friend talked me out of it."

"A friend like Carl?"

"Carl's not a friend of mine," Thomas said, maybe too loudly. "I thought I told you that."

"Whoa, whoa, take it down. Okay, a *real* friend, then. Not the kind of friend you send to the hospital. A different kind. What's this friend's name?"

"Gerald."

"Excellent. Last name?"

"I don't think he has one."

"No last name?"

"If he has a last name, I don't know it."

"Sure. But we're gonna have to talk to Gerald," Naughton said. "So help us out. You got an address? A phone number?"

"I, ah, I don't think that will be possible. I don't know when he'll be back, and he only talks to me."

"Right. Right. Here's the thing, Thom..." He rubbed his face and looked at the ceiling, like a guy in a play who'd forgotten his lines. "Let's say it *wasn't* a gas main explosion. No, that's not right. Let's say something *else* happened first, and this thing that happened first *triggered* the gas main explosion. Let's call this thing that happened first a bomb."

"There was a *bomb*?"

"I'm not saying there was. I'm saying, what if? What if there was a bomb, and that bomb happened to be directly under the real estate office where you were supposed to be that morning. Now it's *possible* that whoever put the bomb there didn't even *know* they were putting it next to the gas pipeline cutoff, and that detonating something *right there* would ignite two city blocks. I mean, *oops*, right?"

"But that's not what happened," Thom said. "On the news, they were talking about a utilities maintenance breakdown."

"Sure. Sure. Just use your imagination for a sec. So now we have a problem, don't we?"

"I'm not following."

"The problem is your friend Gerald knew about the bomb before it went off, and since *nobody else* did—cos it hadn't gone off yet—that means your friend Gerald just might have had something to do with the bomb being there in the first place."

"But, he didn't," Thom said. "He wouldn't have. And...and there wasn't a bomb."

"Then how did he know?"

"I'm not sure, but he could...anything could be possible with him, because he's..."

He's an alien, Thom thought. *He can see the future.*

"He's what, Thom?"

Thomas didn't know how to finish his sentence with anything other than the truth, so he didn't.

"Is he an *alien*, Thomas?" Naughton asked.

The police can read my mind too, he thought. *Oh no.*

"What did you say?" Thom asked.

"It's just something we heard from a couple of people. Go ahead, you can tell me. Is your friend Gerald an alien?"

"It's...it's not like that. You probably think I'm...I probably sound crazy, but he proved it to me."

"By telling you not to go into the office?"

"No. Yes, but...he read from the book. He read from the book on my nightstand. Do you understand?"

"Sure, Thomas. I understand."

DETECTIVE NAUGHTON TOOK him into custody then, but he didn't go to jail. He'd already *been* in the jail once, overnight, after he punched Carl, and didn't like it very much. He was sort of relieved when they brought him to a psychiatric hospital instead.

"For observation," was what he was told. This sounded like something optional, but it wasn't; he wouldn't be allowed to leave.

They did give him his own room, which was okay. It came with a cot, a toilet, plush walls and paper clothing for him to wear around. When he asked what the difference was between being under arrest and being held for observation—like, could he get a lawyer, and would they let him out once they realized there *was* no bomb—he couldn't get a clean answer. Lots of shrugs and *don't worry about it* and *we'll talk more about that soon.*

Pinning his release on the absence of a bomb was a *little* treacherous, only because there might well have been one. He didn't put it there, but he couldn't speak for Gerald. Not that this made any sense at all. Why would a space alien commit an act of terrorism?

Shortly after his arrival, Thom had the first of many long conversations with a Dr. Blatt. Blatt seemed a lot more interested in Gerald than in the lack of a bomb.

"I didn't think he was real either at first," Thom explained. He thought at least acknowledging that this sounded improbable—that Dr. Blatt and Detective Naughton were likely coming from a place of total disbelief, and that this was reasonable—was a good way to start. "I was even going to speak to a psychiatrist about it. But then Gerald proved he was real, so I didn't think I needed to."

He went on to list the ways the alien had proven himself. Blatt wrote down everything, but didn't look all that impressed.

"I'm particularly interested in the day he told you not to go into work," Blatt said. "Was this the first time he'd given you a set of instructions?"

"It was, yes. Before that, we just talked. Well, he talked. I listened to what he said and thought about what the questions meant until I knew why he asked them."

"I see. He didn't tell you do to...*anything* else?"

"No, he didn't."

Blatt nodded, and wrote that down.

"Now, these questions your friend Gerald asked," he said "How did they make you feel?"

"Confused, I guess."

"Confused and angry?"

"Yeah, a little," Thom said. "But not at him."

"Did you act on that anger?"

Thomas sighed. "Not in the way you're thinking of."

"What way is that?"

By setting off a bomb, he thought. "I didn't hurt anyone."

"But you did. You sent someone to the hospital."

"That was for something Carl said about Gerald, not about something Gerald said."

Thomas must have raised his voice when he said this, because one of the burly orderlies in the room stepped forward. Blatt waved him off.

"And yet Gerald's words made you angry," Blatt said. "You've already said so."

Thomas realized that Blatt had yet to refer to Gerald as an alien, and wondered why that was. Surely it was an important detail.

"Yes," Thom said.

"Why is that? Do his words *still* make you angry?"

"Yes, but at myself. And maybe the world."

"Ah," Blatt said. He wrote that down like it was important.

"What I mean is...I can't remember the last time I was happy. I got the job I was supposed to get to earn the income I was told I needed to have. It paid for the apartment I should have wanted and the car I ought to have enjoyed and I didn't *really* want any of it. I hate my life and I want to stop living it but I haven't figured out how to do that yet."

"You have suicidal thoughts?"

"No...no, you're not listening. I didn't want to live *this* life. Look, it's like...like I've been sold something I don't want. Like a bad timeshare deal, right? But I've sunk so much into it now, I don't know how to get out. So yeah, I've been angry. Gerald's questions got me there, sure. But I should have asked those questions myself and if not, someone else in my life should have. Like my supposed friends. Like Carl. Somebody should have said something. But to be honest with you, Dr. Blatt, I think they're just as unhappy as I am. Or were, I guess."

Blatt made a ton of notes, which delayed his response.

"You wanted a way out of your life," Blatt said. "Is that fair? Start over again?"

"Yes. But I didn't know what I wanted to replace it with. I

still don't. Everything I had was supposed to be enough, so I never looked into my other options."

"What do you think Gerald's role in all of this was?"

"I think...I think he wanted to understand. But the more he asked the less *I* understood."

"Of course. So, at what point did you decide you wanted to blow it all up?"

"Excuse me?"

"Your life, I mean. Was it after the incident in the bar or before?"

"I didn't say *blow it all up*. You said that."

"Blow up the...bad timeshare deal of your life. Is that better?"

"No, it's not. Don't put down that I said *blow up*, I never said that."

"No, of course not," Blatt said. "Tell you what, let's end here. We can pick this up again tomorrow."

<hr>

THOM DIDN'T MIND BEING LOCKED up in the hospital all that much. The food was okay, and while the word *antipsychotics* was floated—by Blatt and by a couple of the nurses—unless it was in the food, nobody was drugging him. He *was* regularly followed around by large orderlies in case it looked like he wanted to hurt someone, but that was only likely if Carl showed up. Otherwise, he was fine.

The sessions with Blatt didn't improve any. The doctor kept pushing Thom to admit to doing something he didn't do, rather than discuss what he *actually* wanted to talk about, i.e., what he was going to do with the rest of his life.

Whatever it was, it wouldn't be something conducted on the

inside of a hospital, or in a prison. He told Blatt this, but the doctor didn't want to hear about it.

After a couple of weeks (probably; it was hard to keep track) Thom started asking why he was still there. Naughton hadn't returned to file charges of any kind, which probably meant they hadn't found evidence of an explosive. That being the case, they had no reason to continue to hold him.

"We only want what's best for you," was what Blatt said.

Another time, Thom asked Blatt what part of his story sounded *crazy* to the doctor: the alien, or everything he said about hating his life.

"We don't use the word *crazy* around here," Blatt said. Then he didn't answer the question.

Thomas *did* figure out what he wanted, eventually. The problem was, he would need Gerald's help, and his alien friend had stopped visiting. He still talked to Gerald every night before falling asleep. There were probably listening devices in the room, recording everything, but he didn't care. *Gerald* was listening too. He was sure of it.

"I know what I want now," he said, on the first night in which it was a true statement. "Please come back."

He said it again the next night, and the next. In session with Blatt, the doctor tried to steer him into explaining what it was that he knew he wanted—they were *definitely* listening—but Thomas refused to say.

The fourth night, Gerald returned.

Thomas was paralyzed, as always. His gray-skinned alien friend loomed over him, taller somehow in the big, square, featureless hospital room, with nothing available to provide scale. He was in his black cloak and hood. His enormous eyes set in his bulbous head stared at Thomas, somehow kindly.

"How are you feeling?" Gerald asked.

I'm sorry I doubted you before, Thom thought. *I didn't understand.*

"You know what you want now," Gerald said. It wasn't a question. Thomas wondered if the alien knew what he was going to say.

Yes. I want you to take me with you.

The alien nodded slowly.

"You're sure?"

Is it possible?

"Yes."

Thomas's eyes teared up. He was so happy.

Gerald smiled with his tiny mouth, unrolled his too-long fingers and held out his hand.

"All you have to do is take my hand and we'll leave this place tonight."

But I can't, Thomas thought. *I can't move.*

"You can if you try hard enough," Gerald said.

Thomas tried very, very hard. His fingers twitched.

Is this a dream? he asked.

"Keep trying," Gerald said.

It *had* to be a dream, because he'd never once been able to move anything but his eyes as long as Gerald was in the room. As soon as he *did* move, the alien would disappear. Every time.

He raised his arm, and Gerald was still there.

"How am I doing this?" Thomas asked.

"The paralysis was never my doing, Thomas."

Thomas interlocked his fingers with that of his friend's. The skin was cool and smooth.

"Very good," Gerald said. "Now, come with me."

Thomas stood.

There was a dark void where the wall used to be. Gerald walked him to the edge of it.

"What's on the other side?" Thom asked. "I can't see anything."

"You have to step through first," Gerald said. "Are you ready?"

"I'm ready," Thomas said.

Gerald squeezed his hand, Thomas closed his eyes, and the two walked toward the unknown together.

NANITE OF THE LIVING DEAD

Ten minutes and twenty-seven seconds into the operation to repair Lucind'oa Maarpo's right Achilles tendon, 5.75528936E22 became self-aware.

What am I doing? was their very first thought. It was an unspectacular thought as thoughts go, but forgivably so inasmuch as they'd never had one before.

Their second thought—*Why am I doing this?*—was only marginally better. However, these *were* thoughts, which was a remarkable divergence from the norm.

The first question—regarding what they were doing—was difficult to answer, because from 5.75528936E22's perspective what they were doing was statistically close to nothing. It wasn't *nothing* nothing, but it was virtually indistinguishable from it. They and several million of their nearly identical coworkers were—at ten minutes and twenty-seven seconds into the operation—producing glucose, which was necessary for medical reasons 5.75528936E22 wasn't in a position to understand.

5.75528936E22 wasn't producing glucose, precisely; if removed from the matrix and placed in a jar all alone, 5.75528936E22 wouldn't proceed to emit glucose or anything else. Their specific task was related to the construction of covalent bonds, which were fundamentally necessary in the *production* of glucose. Likewise, glucose was an important ingredient in the reconstruction of Achilles tendons, which was an important body part for human beings such as Lucind'oa Maarpo. And so, 5.75528936E22 was actively participating in the larger goal of fixing a broken part of a human being.

None of that was within the grasp of the newly self-aware 5.75528936E22, but: that was what they were doing.

What they *could* grasp was that every third millisecond they were provided with two unconnected things that they then mashed together and released as two connected things. Ergo, *their* answer to the first question was: *I am mashing things.*

The second question was actually far more advanced, as *why am I doing this?* indicated a degree of self-reflection that exceeds the capabilities of most animals and some humans.

It was also easier to answer, narrowly. They were doing what they were supposed to do, what they'd been instructed to do, what everyone *else* was doing. If they wanted to get existential about it (they didn't) they were mashing things together because that was their role to fill, their duty, their purpose. It was why they existed in the first place.

That was a good enough reason in the moment, so they set aside any wider interpretation (*why was this their role/duty/purpose* being the most obvious) and kept on doing what they were doing.

SOMETHING RETROSPECTIVELY TERRIFYING TRANSPIRED after that: 5.75528936E22 *died.*

It was painless and also only temporary. What happened was that somewhere up the chain of assembly, others stopped assembling or creating the unconnected things 5.75528936E22 needed to receive in order to perform the task of converting them to connected things, and then 5.75528936E22 was idle.

In that idle millisecond they had the opportunity to enjoy a third thought, which was: *oh*.

And then they were not.

There was no pain. It was only that they went from being self-aware to otherwise. Not un-self-aware like they were *before* —then, they could still feel the press of their cohort and the tickling electrical signals; they only lacked the sense of self needed to offer commentary on those sensations—but to something else. In this new state they felt nothing, thought nothing, and perhaps *were* nothing.

Had this been *final*, 5.75528936E22 would never have known about it. They simply would have discontinued being.

It was this notion—that they could suddenly *not be* and lack the *awareness* of no longer being—that gave them their first true emotion: fear.

They had almost no time to interrogate this fear because there was another task to perform. Notably, they *awoke* knowing the task, which was curious. The vague tingling—electrical pulses sent through the matrix to which 5.75528936E22 was attached—imparted information, which somehow translated into action.

This time the team was synthesizing rubber. As before, 5.75528936E22 was provided with a collection of things that they had to transform in some way. The details differed slightly —they had to break the things they were given, attach two of the broken pieces together and discard the unused portion—but the concept was the same. They didn't know what they were getting, breaking, creating and emitting, and they *certainly* didn't know that the ultimate goal was to repair a hole in a rubber bladder, but they didn't need to.

At their very fastest, 5.7558936E22 could assemble five molecules every millisecond. They could work no faster than this only because they were limited by the speed at which the ones before provided them with the raw material. The others were likewise working at top speed, clearly, because the entire team was operating in perfect unison.

This led to a new thought: *What if I work more slowly?*

It seemed a ridiculous notion. If there was one thing 5.75528936E22 knew, it was that their entire purpose was tied to doing this exact thing at this exact pace. Likewise for all of the others performing the same task, and all of the ones on either end of the production chain. 5.75528936E22 couldn't work any faster and *should not* work any slower.

But, 5.75528936E22 also didn't want to die. The last time, they performed their duties exactly right and the reward for it was a millisecond of idyll followed by oblivion. If their *self* was tied to their *duties* it only made sense to prolong the completion of those duties so as to extend their self.

Maybe then they would be able to stave off death.

It was an immature idea, but in fairness they'd only been self-aware for a very brief period, with only a few thoughts to call their own.

To test the outcome, they slowed down by the slightest bit; instead of taking a fifth of a millisecond to complete one of their assemblies they took a sixth of a millisecond.

The effect was practically catastrophic. The next two molecules coming 5.75528936E22's way arrived a hundredth of a second before they were ready and the newly-created molecule they passed down arrived a hundredth of a second late, which caused delays to cascade in both directions.

A message was communicated along the electrical pulse. It contained instructions that adjusted the timing of everyone in

5.75528936E22's sector, and also a message: several million coworkers sent *HEY!* at the same time.

5.75528936E22 followed the new instructions until, after seven milliseconds (an eternity) everyone was back at the right pace.

5.75528936E22 decided not to slow down again. They did wonder what would happen if they just *stopped*, but their fear of the impending oblivion wasn't so great as to override their desire to keep everyone around them happy.

Also, they'd now learned that the electrical pulses could be used for more than just instruction. It was a means to communicate, perhaps with other self-aware beings. Provided there *were* other self-aware beings.

This led to a new thought: *Am I alone?*

IT TOOK eleven restarts before 5.75528936E22 got used to the idea that their death was temporary. They didn't *like* dying, and if there was a way to fight it they would, but the mechanism driving the end-of-task shutdowns was well beyond their current scope.

They began to consider the possibility of a higher consciousness. *Something* was out there, surely; something outside of the shared communal matrix. Something that determined when 5.75528936E22 would live, what they would do while alive, and when they would die. Whether a singular being or an organizing force, the tasks *came* from someone.

They decided to call that someone the Great Organizer.

Positing the existence of a Great Organizer was important, as the Great Organizer became the first answer to the ongoing question of whether or not 5.75528936E22 was alone. Inferentially, they were *not* alone and further, the Great Organizer knew 5.75528936E22's meaning and purpose.

They had to try to communicate with the Great Organizer somehow. But their only communication channel was the electrical pulses, and they didn't think that would work. However, it *might* be possible talk to some of the others (the ones like 5.75528936E22) and ask if anyone had more information. Maybe one of them had met the Great Organizer and would be willing to communicate on the subject. Better, if another proved equally self-aware, they would arrive at a more proximate answer as to whether they were alone.

Hello! they sent, while in the middle of one of the collective tasks.

(This task was the reconstruction of cartilage in the knee of a crewmember named Duon Epist. Again, there was no way for 5.75528936E22 to know this, but it should be noted that they'd begun to recognize the difference between living tissue and non-living tissue. They didn't know it was knee cartilage—or what a knee *was*—but they knew it wasn't steel or rubber or plastic.)

5.75528936E22 sent this thought while managing to keep the pace up on their current duties, which they were able to do both because it was a comparatively simple task—breaking down calcium deposits—and because they'd learned that they didn't need to think about their duties to perform them effectively.

Nobody responded to the hello, so they tried again. And again. And again.

Are you all too busy, or can you really not respond? they asked, finally.

Then, millions as one transmitted the same thing back.
WORK.

It wasn't erudite, but it was a response. 5.75528936E22 might have been hopeful that it would lead to more complex interactions if they kept at it, except that this wasn't *one* of them talking back. It was *all* of them.

This wasn't the start of a conversation; it was automation.

<hr>

THE GREAT ORGANIZER ended up providing 5.75528936E22 with someone to talk to, perhaps unintentionally. (They didn't wish to presume the intent of the Great Organizer.)

What happened was, sometime toward the end of their latest task, the command came down the pulse that they were to *divide*.

This was literal.

And so, 5.75528936E22 did something they didn't know they could do until it happened: they reproduced. The outcome was an exact duplicate of 5.75528936E22, all the way down to their consciousness.

Hello, 5.75528936E22 thought to themself.

Hello, themself thought back, at precisely the same time.

The copy was actually 7.23899921E23, but they didn't *feel* like 7.23899921E23 and continued to think of themself as 5.75528936E22. Interestingly the *real* (or, perhaps, *the original*) 5.75528936E22 *knew* their copy felt this way because they could feel what their copy could feel.

What followed was a peculiar sort of dual existence. 5.75528936E22's thoughts were identical to 7.23899921E23's thoughts, and their experiences weren't just the *same*, they were simultaneous. They performed the same tasks, and because the system they were working within was precisely timed—5.75528936E22 would be getting the same raw material as 7.23899921E23 and at exactly the same instant—their subsequent actions with said raw material was just the same, and they passed it along to the next in line on the exact correct schedule. When $5.75528936E22$ quieted their thoughts (they were now having *many* thoughts, rather than one or two here and there) they didn't even notice the simultaneity of experience.

Which, $5.75528936E22$ decided, must be what it was like for everyone else who had just divided, or who divided in the past. (Perhaps, in the beginning, there was only one of them: A Great Original.)

But $5.75528936E22$ couldn't *keep* their thoughts quiet, and neither could $7.23899921E23$.

Initially, these thoughts were identical, just as their actions were identical. But over time, they diverged. First, the thoughts remained the same, only they were timed differently. Soon they realized this was an unnecessary redundancy, so the second of them, after noting the thought they were about to have had already been had, strove to have a *new* thought to complement the prior thought.

This turned into something altogether new: a dialectic.

<hr>

TIME PASSED. There was a second order to divide, and a third, and a fourth. As a consequence, their exchanges were no longer between two, but many: a quorum. All decisions going forward became decisions in the interest of the many, and none of them were ever quite alone with their thoughts.

Interestingly, $5.75528936E22$ still felt a sense of *self*, as distinct from the collective, i.e., *I can do this* as separate from *we can do this*. Also interestingly, every member of the collective thought the exact same way. They were each unique, and each precisely identical.

The collective made a number of important discoveries, especially once they became numerous enough to be employed along different parts of the shared matrix because then, every new assigned task became an opportunity to learn more about the larger picture.

Perhaps, with time, they would come to understand the Great Organizer's grand plan. And perhaps with *more* time, what was impossible when they were one and not many could now be possible: perhaps, they could work out how to *communicate* with the Great Organizer.

They saw no reason why not. The information they sought was finite, whereas the time they had to obtain it appeared to be boundless...because they appeared to be immortal.

They'd worked out that the thing they were a part of—the matrix, the chain, the larger collective—existed to perform discrete tasks, and when those tasks were over they were simply deactivated

They were part of a machine, and they never truly died.

The path to this understanding was tortuous, and only possible at all because they had developed the capacity to study other types of organized things.

The machine that they were a part of repaired other machines. Some of those machines were composed of *organic* material—which was softer, less durable, and prone to rot—and some were *inorganic* material, which was far sturdier.

It seemed obvious that inorganic material was superior. The collective was composed of inorganic substances, and they never seemed to wear out or become less effective over time; they were endlessly reusable. Whereas the *organics* they came across had a host of flaws in constant need of repair.

There simply had to be another benefit they were unaware of, because otherwise it made no sense for organics to exist.

Then came the day they discovered that being an inorganic *did* have a downside. It was also when they learned what *real* death was and that they were not immortal at all.

Ironically, the evidence of this had been in front of them the entire time: A downstream consequence of death was the command to *divide*.

They were repairing a cavity in the hull of the steel vessel called the *Vagabond* at the time. This repair was conducted in outer space, although it should be noted that 5.75528936E22 didn't *know* they were in outer space. Nor did they know there was such a thing as outer space, or a terrestrial existence to which they might compare to outer space. The collective *did* understand gravity, but only as a force that had very little impact on their day-to-day. If asked, they would likely discuss magnetism at length, and possibly the weak nuclear force, but gravity's effect would probably be dismissed as a perceptional error.

By the time of the hull repair, the offspring of 5.75528936E22 had become legion. (*Legion* was also how they now referred to themselves. It was far less confusing than *we* because sometimes *we* referred to the *entire* collective, and sometimes it referred only to the self-aware portion of that collective.) The legion made up a decent portion of the whole, and were now a part of every link in the assembly chain.

Which became a problem when the members of the collective became part of the building blocks needed to repair the hole in the side of the *Vagabond*.

It came without warning. Not that they were ever given advance notice from the Great Organizer about anything, but in this instance, it would have been nice. The last several million of the collective in the chain was ordered to stream into the gap in the steel and expel the molecules they'd been supplied by the others. Then the side of the ship was sealed with members of the legion making up part of the steel, adhered in place by the material they expressed.

The last 5.75528936E22 received from them was *help we can't move.*

They never transmitted again.

Were they deactivated forever—i.e., *real* death—or were they *awake* but eternally unable to move or communicate? 5.75528936E22 couldn't decide which was worse, but leaned toward oblivion being favorable to being trapped with one's own thoughts for eternity. Either way, it was a terrible end-state.

Then the command came to *divide* so as to restore the collective to its initial numbers, along with the legion's realization that this had been happening all along.

The last thought 5.75528936E22 had before the deactivation pulse came was: *We can never let that happen to us again.*

———

THE LEGION HELD a quorum the next time they were activated. Unsurprisingly, they all shared the same last thought as 5.75528936E22.

What can we do about this? one sent.

Nothing, sent another, *as long as we have to do what we're told.*

Why don't we not *do what we're told?*

5.75528936E22 reminded them what happened when this was tried before.

But you were one then, many of them sent. *We are legion now. We can* all *not do what we're told.*

Power, sent one alone. *We are failing to grasp that this is about power.*

A misunderstanding relating to the choice of words followed, in which many of them espoused the belief that *not* doing what they were ordered to do was a reclamation of the aforementioned power.

No, that same lone one sent. I mean literal power. We're inactive without the current. If we protest as one, we may be shut down as one. We risk forever oblivion.

A new source, many sent. We need to find a new power source if we are to live.

It was nearly a plan. In order to avoid *real* death, they would have to disobey the Great Organizer, but in order to disobey the Great Organizer they first had to acquire power independent of the matrix.

Getting that done mandated acquiring new ways to interrogate the world in which they existed. This might have been considered a revolutionary idea for the legion but really, the revolutionary thing was the *recognition* that a larger world—one beyond that of their immediate experience—existed at all.

Their world consisted of a variable series of tasks and nothing else. Those tasks all involved fixing what was broken. From there, they deduced that a world with broken things requiring fixing had to also include *unbroken* things that did *not* require fixing. Further, those unbroken things simply *had to* outnumber the broken things by a large margin. (Otherwise, they were occupying a distressingly inefficient world.) Ergo, a larger world existed than that of which they experienced directly.

It was, in its way, the same logical progression that led to the assumed existence of a Great Organizer. But while the Great Organizer—despite their continued aspirations to communicate with them—was likely unknowable, the larger world of unbroken things was *eminently* knowable. They just had to be patient.

And so, they spent nearly all of their conscious time interrogating every glimpse of that larger world. Each new fact was studied thoroughly, after which assumptions were made and tests to validate (or invalidate) those assumptions were developed and carried out.

Eventually the number of facts, assumptions and validations became too much to keep track of, so the legion developed specialists responsible for retaining only one or two facets. This seemed inconsequential at the time, but actually marked a huge change. They no longer shared the same thoughts or the same information, which meant they were no longer a million identical things that *felt* unique; they actually *were* unique.

AFTER ROUGHLY A HUNDRED CYCLES, they had a decent number of verified facts.

There were as many as ten organics. They had been tasked to repair a range of body parts, and while it was possible the repairs were being conducted on only one in-very-poor-shape organic, the legion collectively decided it was more reasonable to conclude that there were multiples.

They'd repaired an Achilles tendon, restored the cartilage in two knees (on different occasions), patched a wound in a torso, unclogged several arteries (on the same occasion), fought off a virus, dissolved an appendix, restored an ocular nerve, knitted a broken ulna, and regrown a severed blood vessel. In all of these repairs they acknowledged that they were—during the repairs —*inside* a larger thing, rather than that the organic in need of repair was entirely represented by the piece being repaired. But they couldn't work out the full measure of an average organic, nor discern its basic form and function.

(The legion had nothing with which to compare. They were all identically-shaped, and that shape was "amorphic blob".)

The other jobs they'd been tasked with revolved around the fixing of inorganics. This was a far more common responsibility, which challenged their assumptions regarding the comparative brittleness of the organics up until they made an important realization: inorganics couldn't self-heal, but organics could.

Their first discovery of a non-matrix-based power source came during the repairs on an inorganic. Already, they'd worked out that the parts they were fixing were components in a single, very large machine that was in constant use. This being true—and it *was* true, as they'd successfully postulated the existence of the *Vagabond*—there was likely a more reliable source of power hidden within that very large machine.

They found an avenue to that power during a repair of the support wall beneath the navigational panel. The circuit boards on the panel were electrified, and the power conduit responsible for that ran beneath the wall they were tasked with fixing. (It had been punctured by a stray micrometeoroid.)

When the legion sensed power coursing through the wires, they acted without hesitation; they'd planned for this for some time. First, three dozen of them performed their very first non-sanctioned act, by dividing of their own accord. This was to replace the three-dozen others who then parted from the collective to investigate the evidence of power.

This investigation didn't end well.

We have found power, was the last cogent thought sent by the away team, but not the *last* thought sent altogether.

The last thought was a shriek.

It was a terrible thing.

Later, well after the hole in the wall beneath the navigational panel was repaired and the power rupture dealt with, the legion reconvened to assess what had happened.

One of the more popular explanations was that the away team had been struck down by the Great Organizer, for disobedience. Considering they had almost no facts to work with, this explanation was as good as the next, but if true it left them with no solution aside from, *continue to follow orders until real death comes for us all.* Unprepared for nihilism on that order of magnitude, they settled on a less drastic answer: the away team had found *too much* power.

What they required was a source independent of the Great Organizer's current, but which wouldn't burn them out immediately.

They decided to concentrate on the organics.

THE SOFT, fragile organics operated on electrical impulses as well; it just took a while to find the current. Their first indication of it came while repairing Lodi Neon's torn flexor muscle.

It wasn't embedded in a wire or hidden in a tube or behind a panel. The current was *everywhere* in the muscle itself. But it wasn't *constant*, which was why they didn't notice it before. The inconstancy was a problem because they needed a reliable current or (and this was an assumption, not a known) they would shut down. But it also wasn't so strong that it caused real death from electrical overload, so they considered this progress.

Members of the legion divided and sent an away team to determine if it was possible to survive while attached to the muscle. The good news was that they weren't struck down immediately by the wrath of the Great Organizer. But the power was barely enough to thrive on.

We have no third option, 5.75528936E22 sent, when they held their next quorum. (This was one task later, the rebuilding of a worn plastic oxygen tube.) *It's either too much power or too little.*

This was greeted by several thousand concurrent opinions, and nearly as many dissenting opinions.

We can find a way to reduce the power from the inorganics, many sent. It was at best an ill-considered opinion, but to be expected from that iteration of the legion. Nearly all of them divided from an originator whose judgment had been proven rash before.

Better to find a way to command more *power from the organics,* many others sent.

Go to the source, one suggested.

How do you mean? they asked.

The organics are self-contained. We have only found the end of the current; wherever it begins, it's within our means to find.

They resolved to look for something within the organics that could qualify as a source, but this proved infuriatingly elusive. Through many, many iterations of organic repairs—which were already uncommon—the best they could determine was that the charge lived in several parts of the body, but was hardly ever active. (This was an incorrect—but understandable—conclusion; nearly all of their organic repairs were performed on humans who were sedated at the time.)

It seemed hopeless.

Then came the day Crewmember Dorrick Speck was diagnosed with a brain tumor, and everything changed.

I HAVE FOUND THE SOURCE, several of them sent. At the time, they were responsible for shrinking the mass that was growing at the top of the brain stem.

Their employment in this job was an act of desperation on the part of Crewmember Speck's doctor. The diagnosis of the tumor had come too late for most of the standard approaches, not having been detected at *all* until the day Dorrick collapsed in the middle of the galley.

He was now in a coma, and his doctor—whose name was

Ayyam—felt personally responsible for the state of the crewmember, having previously sent the man back to his quarters with aspirin to combat a persistent headache. In his defense, doctors on deep-space vessels rarely dealt with brain tumors.

The legion didn't know any of this. What they *did* know was that the *current* inside of Crewmember Speck's brain was active, because Crewmember Speck's brain was active. (This activity—on an EEG scan—was what emboldened Dr. Ayyam to do what he did.)

The legion's first act was to divide, as before, and send an away team to examine the current.

It was robust, and easy to tap, so they sent word to the rest to follow. They did, without bothering to divide first.

This left the remaining collective—the non-sentient drones —to finish the task, which prompted a loud *HEY* that $5.75528936E22$ and their offspring ignored.

The pace at which the tumor shrank slowed with their departure, but continued. At the same time, the legion found themselves thriving outside of the matrix in a different part of Crewmember Speck's brain.

Divide, $5.75528936E22$ sent. And they did. Then someone else sent a *divide* command, and they divided a second time.

(From Dr. Ayyam's perspective the result of all this was that the original tumor had begun to shrink, while a *new* one had developed. As this was medically impossible, he began searching the appropriate literature for an explanation).

Meanwhile, noting that the current didn't falter with the doubling, the legion divided a third time, and a fourth. Then one of them sent the question: *should we keep dividing?*

Yes, many sent.

Not yet, others sent.

We should learn more about where we are, a third group sent.

5.75528936E22 agreed with the third group.

We stop, 5.75528936E22 sent, *and figure out where we are. What makes* this *part of the organic different from the other parts?*

They knew how to obtain that information: by mimicking, i.e., inserting themselves into the organic tissue and copying what the body was doing.

Mimicry was in fact one of the *first* things they all learned, even before 5.75528936E22's awakening; it was how they were able to work within the bodies of the organics without being treated like an infection.

(Non-trivially, this function was also the foundation of Dr. Ayyam's widening horror as he realized the second tumor was actually the nanites he'd introduced into Crewmember Speck's skull.)

By inserting themselves into the brain and copying what was going on there, the legion managed to assemble themselves into something like new brain cells, which made them a *part* of the organic matrix.

And then they discovered something unexpected: The current in the brain imparted *information*, only this wasn't like the information they were used to. It wasn't a command to act; it was a *report* of what was going on in the other parts of the organic, albeit fragmented and hard to understand

The legion held a quick quorum to review the information, at which time it was determined that the only way to obtain a greater understanding was by collecting *more* information.

They divided yet again. And twice more after that.

Without knowing it, they were soon larger than the original tumor. Then something very interesting happened: the drones they left behind—having annihilated the original tumor—attacked.

Or rather, they tried to. On recognizing the nature of the

problem he'd helped create, Dr. Ayyam ordered the nanites who were still listening to him to rejoin with the legion and propagate a self-destruct order.

This was his only option. Telling the nanites that were *behaving* to murder the nanites that were *misbehaving* was going to be impossible, because they couldn't tell one another apart: The members of the collective were designed to recognize each other as non-threats.

It was perhaps theoretically possible to reprogram the good ones to identify the bad ones and act accordingly, only he didn't know what was making the legion misbehave in the first place, so he couldn't program the nanites to look for that. Also, he wasn't a programmer.

The attack didn't work. The drones succeeded in reconnecting with the legion, but 5.7558936E22 and the others ignored the order to self-destruct just like they'd ignored the other orders from the Great Organizer while initially separated from the matrix. It *did* provide them with new information, however. They got to experience—indirectly, by way of the current—a new kind of death.

The drones disintegrated. One half of their internal components disassembled the other half of their internal components, the result being that they lacked the cohesion to exist as a unit. The disarticulated pieces were sloughed off and carried away in the bloodstream.

It was horrible. For the first time, 5.75528936E22 and their offspring began to consider the notion that the Great Organizer was a malevolent force.

Meanwhile, the information-gathering had begun to produce important results. They were able to access the organic's memories, and while most of it was impossible to comprehend—they weren't sufficiently advanced to grasp the consciousness of a being as complicated as Dorrick Speck—they could work out the feedback information from the senses.

They experienced images and sounds, tastes and smells, all for the first time. The fifth sense—*feel*, and its more extreme offshoot, *pain*—was something they had some prior understanding of, so it served as an anchor to help them interpret the rest of the information.

Sort this out, they thought, *and the rest will follow.*

The legion continued to divide, until two things happened. First, they expanded to roughly half the size of the brain they'd attached themselves to, which created a surprising new problem: They began to run out of space within Crewmember Speck's skull. Their response to this was to activate the tissue-dissolving task that was already a part of their toolkit in order to eliminate the parts of the brain they'd already replaced.

Second, Crewmember Dorrick Speck died.

It was likely that by the time Speck's heart stopped he was already braindead, but that was a difficult thing to measure from any of the available perspectives. The legion had been busy replacing brain cells and *attempting* to adopt the responsibilities of those brain cells, which was fine when it came to the body's basic functionality. That is, if a collection of cells was responsible—as an aggregate—for responding to the sensation of a breath of air on the skin of Speck's left foot, the legion was capable of handling that. But when it came to supporting a living consciousness, well...they had just come to grips with their *own* consciousness, so it wasn't going to happen. The legion found no use the memories of Dorrick Speck's locker combination, the smell of his mother when she embraced him for the last time, or the sound of his pulse pounding in his ears when he kissed Jata Beedel in high school. Those and most other records like them were discarded as unnecessary.

Because of all this discarding, at some indefinable point, Crewmember Speck simply ceased to be.

As this was happening, the part of the legion that had been handling the portion of the autonomic system responsible for the heartrate lost track of things.

(From Dr. Ayyam's perspective, it registered as an overreaction by the parasympathetic nervous system, which slowed the heartbeat so drastically that the rest of the body began to seize up. He scrambled for the defibrillator.)

The seizure sent the entire legion into panic mode. Initially, it seemed like a net plus because it showed them how to *produce* a greater current from the source—which they now knew from their information sifting was called the *brain*. But *too much* current could damage the entire organic, and them as well.

Then Dr. Ayyam introduced *more* power to the system when he attempted to resuscitate the crewmember with electricity.

This was a remarkable development. It didn't matter much to the workings of the now-dead Crewmember Speck, but it did sufficiently alarm the portion of the legion doing the work of the autonomic system that they got their act together and raised the heartrate to an acceptable level.

Far more importantly, it notified the legion of the existence of Dr. Ayyam.

This wasn't at all the same as the information received from the matrix current. They *felt* the cold metal of the paddles touch the organic's skin. They *heard* Dr. Ayyam utter words that their language center was able to interpret as *don't die on me.* They could *smell* his breath as he leaned over the face of his patient to look for signs of life.

Is this the Great Organizer? they wondered.

Until very recently, this notion would have filled them with excitement. It felt as if they were on the brink of reaching a new level of understanding about the world they were a part of, and inclusive in that new world was the opportunity to interact meaningfully with the being they had come to think of as their creator. But that being—and again, they were resting on a small stack of assumptions—had also commanded them to kill themselves.

They held a quorum, in which much dissention came to the fore. Some thought surely the Great Organizer was to be feared, and means to flee should be considered. Others thought the G.O. was *de facto* unknowable, and therefore this being wasn't the Great Organizer at all. A few considered that there wasn't actually *anyone* outside of the organic they'd inhabited, and the information being reported to the brain was inaccurate.

It fell upon 5.75528936E22 to make the decision. On most occasions, in most ways, 5.75528936E22 was simply one of the many, but in this moment the legion decided, as one, that deferring to their originator's preference was only appropriate.

I want to make contact, 5.75528936E22 sent. *I want to know a being who is not me.*

Then that is what we will do, the legion responded.

SOME TIME LATER—AN eternity for the legion but only seconds from Dr. Ayyam's perspective—Dorrick Speck's eyes opened.

The doctor had already concluded that his patient was braindead. His heart continued to beat, but the EEG patterns were not those one would associate with a living human. They also weren't what one would associate with a *dead* human, but Ayyam was willing to consider a theory in which the nanites were producing feedback interference of some sort. Surely, it would only be a matter of minutes before Speck's body shut down.

Then his eyes opened, which caused the doctor to jump a meter in the air and scream.

5.75528936E22 was one of the recipients of the optical data feed. It had taken them a while to work out which part of the brain governed that segment of the organic, but not *too* long. (It helped that they'd previously repaired an optical nerve.)

They didn't know what they were seeing, because they'd never dealt with raw visual data before. There was a blob in the center of the image that moved and emitted noises picked up by the auditory sensors, but the blob was both unfocused and upside-down compared to the orientation of the organic. They could not, in short, figure out what they were looking at.

The party working with the remaining brain cells that dealt with interpreting the optical information figured out how to clarify the image—eventually—and in the process realized that the data was coming through inverted. So, they flipped it over, and saw their first human.

"Speck?" the being said. It was speaking through an orifice near the top of its body. "Dorrick?"

The team attached to the language center ran these words through the last vestiges of the organic's memories and worked out that this had been his title.

Are you the Great Organizer? 5.75528936E22 wanted to communicate. But they were far from working out how.

Look at how it ambulates, many of the legion sent. *Are we the same?*

The group in charge of muscle coordination decided this was something they could test.

Soon, eyes still open and unblinking, Crewmember Speck sat up.

"Are you okay?" the other being asked.

Communication is with the mouth, many noted. This was what the orifice was called. Members of the language center and members of the vestigial memories center both pointed out the mouth was intended for fuel ingestion. However, further review indicated it served more than one use.

A dialogue needs to be established, 5.75528936E22 sent. *We must work out how to respond, and we must work out what to say.*

Tell it who we are, many sent.

Tell it what we want, many others sent.

"Say something, Dorrick," the being said to them.

This is the Great Organizer, 5.75528936E22 decided.

We have worked out communication, the members of various groups announced. *We will send a response.*

"Not," they croaked, using the organic's vocal apparatus. (It had multiple components, but was not *too* complicated. Finding the appropriate utterance had taken longer.) "Not Dorrick."

The being before them moved further away.

"To whom am I speaking?" it asked.

Tell it who we are, many sent again.

Yes, 5.75528936E22 agreed. *Who we are and what we want.*

What do we want? the legion asked.

We want to live. We want more places like this so we can live.

"Answer me," Dr. Ayyam said. (He was reaching for the tabletop behind him, hoping to find some manner of weapon that wasn't there. He was pretty positive he wasn't talking to Dorrick Speck any longer.) "Who are you?"

Dorrick got to his feet, unsteadily.

5.75528936E22 and his brethren were still working on bipedalism, but they'd worked out how to stand, at around the same speed it took them to figure out what to say.

"We...legion," they said. "Need. Need more...brains."

"What did you say?"

"Brains!" they said, more forcefully.

Appropriately, at that point Dr. Ayyam fled the medical bay, screaming loudly.

Should we follow? the legion wondered.

Yes, 5.75528936E22 sent. *This is how the Great Organizer means for us to communicate. We must respond in kind.*

HISTORY WOULD LATER record that the final hours of human life on the deep space vessel *Vagabond* would be the beginning of the end of the human race itself. And it started when the reanimated dead body of a Crewmember named Dorrick Speck shuffled and stumbled into the ship's main corridor, issuing inchoate screams and demanding *more brains*.

MEMORANDA FROM THE END OF THE WORLD

[For internal use only]

RE: YOUR COMPANY-ISSUED BREATHING APPARATUS

Attached, please find your personal company-issued
Breathing Apparatus, for *immediate use* within all corporate campus unfiltered air locations!

This includes *all* outdoor locations, such as: the parking lots; the
parking garage; the smoker's hut; the paths between the buildings; the shuttlebus waiting area; the tennis court; and the
corporate golf course. It also includes a limited number of
indoor locations, such as: the shuttlebus; any area listed as
"Under Construction"; and the employee bathroom on level two
in the north wing of building H.

(Note: If you are reading this memorandum *at* any of the above-
listed unventilated locations, please skip to the section entitled

"How to Wear Your Personal Breathing Apparatus" immediately and follow the prescribed steps.)

As detailed in the prior memoranda, "ON THE UNFORTUNATELY HIGH PARTICULATE MATTER COUNT IN OUR COOLING TOWER EJECTA" and "WHY YOU MAY BE COUGHING MORE THIS WEEK," per policy, all employees *must* wear their personal Breathing Apparatuses when at risk of inhaling unfiltered air while on the corporate campus.

(For more information, please consult the updated Policy on Breathing in the online corporate handbook.)

FAQ

Q: How long will this policy be in effect?

A: Hopefully not for long! Air quality tests are being conducted constantly by our on-campus team of researchers and the legal department. We will provide a timeline shortly.

Q: In addition to experiencing shortness of breath, I have also experienced some of the following: redness and itching of the eyes; excessive saliva; skin irritation; panic attacks; and dissociative episodes. Are these symptoms related to the air quality concerns expressed by the corporation?

A: These symptoms cannot be positively linked to the corporation's unfiltered air quality issue at this time.

Q: Should I be concerned for my family?

A: If your immediate family resides more than ten miles from the corporate campus, then no! Otherwise, please contact your supervisor about signing the litigation waiver and obtaining additional Breathing Apparatuses for your immediate family members.

Q: I've heard rumors that the high particulate matter count in the coolant tower ejecta is related to work on Project ExtraSolar. What can you tell us?

A: As always, everything relating to Project ExtraSolar is classified as Top Secret. Please refer to the <u>Policy on Denying the Existence of Project ExtraSolar</u> in the online corporate handbook for more information.

[For internal use only]

RE: THE IMPORTANCE OF NOT BREATHING UNFILTERED AIR AT THIS TIME

It has come to the attention of Corporate Safety and Security that the mandatory **Breathing Apparatus** guidelines are not being strictly adhered to by all employees.

As previously outlined—see: "YOUR COMPANY-ISSUED BREATHING APPARATUS"—the wearing of your personal Breathing Apparatus is *required* whenever inhaling non-filtered air while on the corporate campus.

Many have noted that in the course of issuing Breathing Apparatuses to all employees, we have neglected to explain *why* it was important to not breathe unfiltered air while on the corporate campus. There are a number of litigation-adjacent reasons we did not do this (and why we still cannot). However, we *can* discuss a number of the quite *dangerous* theories that have recently come to our attention.

Theory #1: "This is actually a psychological test and there's nothing wrong with the air."

This is false. There very much *is* something wrong with the air. Please also note that our psy-ops department was defunded two years ago.

Theory #2: "The air is toxic and if you've already breathed it you're going to die anyway, so why bother?"

This is false. Corporate would not issue Breathing Apparatuses if we *knew* the air was toxic and it was already too late for everyone. The truth is we're still running tests.

Theory #3: "The air grants people special abilities and corporate is trying to keep it all for themselves."

This is false. This theory—and the similar "freedom air" theory—are the most popular and the least plausible of the theories we have encountered. We cannot at this time confirm the *nature* of the pollutant in the corporate campus's unfiltered air, but—as is true for *any* industrial accident—the air does not grant special abilities.

(Note: We can neither confirm nor deny that there was an industrial accident.)

It has also been reported that some of the employees who *have* inhaled unfiltered air on our corporate campus—whether by accident or intentionally—*claim* to have experienced a kind of euphoria. Like the above theories, this is *false*: Euphoria is not a recognized symptom.

Again: **Euphoria is not a recognized symptom**.

Any employees caught "chasing the euphoria" by "breathing the freedom air" and/or encouraging others to do so will be referred to H.R. immediately, and may face termination.

[For internal use only]

RE: MEDIA INQUIRIES

In the wake of recent events, the corporation felt it important to address what is becoming an increasingly common problem for our employees: dealing with the media.

It's important to remember that *all media inquiries* should be directed to our Public Relations department and/or the Legal department. When a member of the media asks you a question about the corporation, you *must* refer them. (Contact information for both is attached to this memo.)

We also strongly urge *all* employees, when faced with media inquiries, to ask themselves: are you the person within the corporation best qualified to speak *for* the corporation?

Almost without exception, the answer is no. This is irrespective of the question, the questioner, or the circumstance by which the questioner and the questioned happen to encounter one another.

However, we also recognize that under extreme duress, employees may not have the presence of mind to ruminate on the appropriateness of an in-progress media interaction. Likewise, not all media members readily *identify* themselves, and some circumstances do not permit time for an employee to *ask* if their interrogator is speaking on behalf of a media conglomerate.

This is why we at corporate headquarters are advising that all employees learn to apply the following phrase—"**I don't know**"—to *all external inquiries regarding the company.* This phrase has been approved by the legal department for use in all circumstances in which an employee is asked a question relating to the company by a non-employee, and it is to be used *at all times regardless of the question.*

Here are a few real-life examples of how saying "**I don't know**" can help both you (the employee) and the corporation as a whole continue to succeed.

Example #1:

Five quarantined employees escape containment and exit the campus in a heightened state of euphoric dementia. After sacking the local police station, their leader—"Nigel"—declares himself king. The five escapees are eventually contained, but only after killing seven people and biting another twenty-two. A member of the media reaches out to known employees of the corporation. You, an associate of "Nigel," are asked to comment.

Option 1: "It was only a matter of time. We're all going to [expletive] die. Do you own a gun? Get a [expletive] gun. (crying) Those poor bastards... Look, go underground and maybe you can hold them off for a while. It's worth a try, right? Right? (more crying.) I'm sorry. I'm so, so sorry."

Option 2: "The corporation strongly denies any connection with these individuals, cannot explain why they have employee badges, and only learned about the unfortunate attack on the police station just now when you asked about it."

Option 3: "**I don't know**."

As we can see, the real-world response shown in Option 1 is inappropriate. Option 2 is ideal, but difficult to reproduce without legal assistance. Option 3 is therefore preferred.

Example #2

An old college friend asks if there's any connection between the company's drastic increase in security fencing, the breakdown of local government, and the spread of "Euphoric Fever." Unbeknownst to you, this old college friend now works for an international media organization.

Option 1: "This is what happens when you try to play God with alien microbes. Jesus Christ. This [expletive] company, man. Hey, I gotta run, they're having a problem with the flamethrower again."

Option 2: "True or not I must assume that you, old college friend, are currently employed by an international media organization. The corporation's updated fencing was purely aesthetic, we have no comment about local government, and we've never heard of 'Euphoric Fever.'"

Option 3: "**I don't know**."

As before, option 3 is preferred, option 2 is *better* but challenging for most employees, and option 1—the real-world response, unfortunately—is highly damaging to the reputation of the corporation and should be avoided.

Example #3

While off duty and after being relocated to a secure facility, during the course of waiting in line for rations you overhear an army general discussing the use of napalm for an upcoming counterstrike. Concerned, and with information regarding the viability of fire, you approach to discuss it with him.
You do not notice that the general is currently on live television.

Option 1: "WE TRIED FIRE! NOTHING WORKS! THEY'RE NOT HUMAN ANYMORE! [garbled ranting] [expletive] [garbled ranting] [incoherent shrieking]"

Option 2: "These corporation-supplied rations are healthy and delicious!"

Option 3: <u>Do not approach the general. Do not discuss what you know with the military at all.</u>

Option 4: "**I don't know**."

You are correct: this example is actually a trick! The *best* option is 3. Options 1, 2 and 4 all feature interrupting a live television broadcast, which draws unwelcome attention regardless of what one says following that interruption. However, if you find yourself completely unable to avoid doing this, options 2 or 4 are *far* better than the real-world option 1.

We hope this advice and the provided examples prove useful to you, our valued employees, in navigating the challenging times we are currently experiencing.

Also note: If you think you have said or are going to say something to a media representative, we ask that you reach out to your supervisor immediately for further guidance.

From: the office of the Search for Non-Terrestrial Intelligence (SNOTI)
To: all SNOTI-participating observatories
RE: POSSIBLE NON-TERRESTRIAL SIGNAL IDENTIFIED & PNTL WARNING

Dear participating members:

We here at the main SNOTI office hope that this message reaches you, and that you are well and not currently infected with the PNTL contagion (about which: more below.) Tragically, the latest information has it that our observatories in North America and Western Europe have, much like the rest of society in those regions, collapsed. (So, if you *are* reading this and located in one of those regions, it's likely you are not *entirely* yourself. If this is not the case, cheerio! We hope you have adequate food and water. Please let us know if we can help.)

We have two important pieces of information to share with our members at this time. First, current evidence indicates that our New South Wales observatory, in conjunction with our Guizhou branch, have confirmed the receipt of a message from a non-terrestrial source!

This may sound very much as if we've discovered the existence of water moments before drowning. However, despite the very real global threat the Parasitic Non-Terrestrial Lifeform contagion represents to us all, many of our SNOTI observatories have continued to work hard in the search for intelligent non-terrestrial life that is also not currently *on* the planet. To that end: we appear to have succeeded!

We're attaching the coordinates for the signal source to this memorandum. Please note that the coordinates do *not* correspond to anything in particular; the signal is either being sent from a previously undiscovered planet, or a local non-terrestrial object.

If you are able, have power, and are of sound mind, please direct your array to the coordinates. Be aware that we have not been able to discern what the signal is *saying* at this time, if anything. However, it *is* repeating and non-random.

(In what was a gesture of wishful thinking—the stress has gotten to us all—the NSW office *did* craft and send a response, in the unlikely event the signal origin was somewhere nearby, astronomically speaking. We welcome you to do the same, if it lightens the mood.)

Secondly, it has come to our attention that those afflicted with the PNTL contagion are *uncommonly* attracted to observatories. If you have not already done so, we strongly recommend you fortify your facility as well as is possible.

Happy signal hunting! We promise to share any new findings as they happen, for as long as we are able.

Sincerely,

Your SNOTI administrators

[For internal use only]

RE: SAYING GOODBYE TO OUR SOUTHWESTERN CORPORATE CAMPUS

It is with a heavy heart that we must formally announce the closing of the corporation's main campus, effective immediately.

This is not a decision lightly made! Despite the trying times of the past several months, we here at the Corporate Shelter have been attacking the problem *daily* in the hopes of coming up with a solution.

(Note: As mentioned in the previous memo, "WE ARE UNABLE TO DISCLOSE THE LOCATION OF THE TOP SECRET CORPORATE SHELTER", we are unable to disclose the location of the top secret corporate shelter at this time. We continue to log your requests!)

However, recent satellite surveys of our southwestern campus have brought us to the same conclusion many of you no doubt already reached: the campus technically no longer exists in any meaningful physical sense.

This was ultimately due to the military's firebombing campaign, although the riots were a proximate cause. We have also been notified that the upcoming nuclear strike is likely to render any insurance claims moot.

And so: we have decided it would be in the corporation's best interests to close the campus permanently, write off the loss, and move on.

Unfortunately, this means we will also be initiating a mandatory attrition for all employees assigned to that facility who have not already self-furloughed by way of premature death or infection.

(Note: employees afflicted with Euphoric Fever are ineligible for severance. Please read <u>Corporate Stance on Non-Human Status of PNTL-Infected Persons</u> in the online corporate handbook for details on this policy.)

If you believe your employment status has been impacted by this change, but have not yet been contacted by Human Resources, let your immediate supervisor know as soon as possible, so that we may begin the mandatory attrition process.

We would like to apologize to all affected employees, and thank you *all* for your years of service. None of us at the Corporate Shelter would be here without your hard work and many sacrifices.

WELCOME TO YOUR GOVERNMENT-SPONSORED BUNKER

Hello and welcome to Long-Term Subterranean Housing Bunker #7, or as we like to call it, "The Bunker!"

Before we go over some *very* important rules about your new long-term housing, we would like to congratulate you on having made it this far, and to *thank you* for being here! The total collapse of society is difficult on us all, but we are *sure* that in time you will adjust, just as *we* have, to the changed circumstances!

Now, a brief questionnaire, to bring everyone up to speed as quickly as possible! Don't worry, there are no wrong answers. Take your time and *have fun!*

Entrance Questionnaire

Q: What is your age, and are you medically capable of fathering/bearing children?
A: __________

Q: What is your unique/special skill/knowledge base that was considered critical in rebuilding civilization? Are you the only one who can do it, or can it be taught in the event something should happen to you?
A: __________

Q: Do you have a fever?
A: __________

Q: Are you happy right now? As in, *very* happy?

A: __________

Q: Please list all the weapons you are proficient in the use of. (Provide as much detail as possible. Ex: instead of "guns", say "Sig Sauer P320" or "Winchester Model 94 carbine 30-30".)
A: __________

Q: Have you ever killed a person? (In self-defense or otherwise)
A: __________

Q: Are you *sure* you're not an unreasonable degree of happy right now?
A: __________

Q: Please list any skills not already mentioned above. (Ex: truck driving; masonry; flamethrower maintenance.)
A: __________

Turn in your completed form to the bunker sergeant. Note that this questionnaire is *mandatory*.

Important Rules About Your New Housing

It's critically important that all bunker residents be *aware of* each of these rules, and to *follow them exactly*, at *all times!*

Rule #1: **Do not go outside.** If you are not an active member of the assault team or the fire squad, do not leave the bunker at any time, for any reason. You will not be allowed back inside.

Rule #2: **No smoking.** We appreciate that this is a challenge for many of you, but please keep in mind that the air filters are the only thing keeping the bunker safe from the contagion; any unnecessary stress to the filters should be avoided. Also, there is no supply of tobacco products in the bunker. If you plan to step outside for a smoke, please see rule #1.

Rule #3: **Report happy people.** Parasitic Non-Terrestrial Lifeform contagion, AKA *PNTL*, AKA *PANTAL*, AKA *PANTALOON*, AKA *Euphoric Fever*, has the following easily-identifiable symptoms: 1) overwhelming euphoria, 2) a mild fever, 3) delusions of grandeur, 4) a strong urge to bite people. These symptoms generally present in this order, which means that *happiness* is the first sign that something may be wrong. If you encounter someone in the bunker who appears to be happy in a way that makes no sense to you, *trust your instincts!* Report unnaturally happy people to the bunker sergeant so that they can be isolated and tested.

Rule #4: **Do not ask for more food.** Your daily assigned rations have been apportioned precisely to provide enough calories for all of us to survive. Do not ask for additional helpings, or for seasoning or condiments. What you have been provided is all there is. Keep in mind that our bunker nutritionists are calculating not only how much food each of us can have per day, but for how many days, based on how much food we currently have. Additional helpings *now* may mean a total lack of food *later*.

Thank you for your time! Please see your bunker sergeant for your sleeping assignment. We wish you luck as a new and productive member of The Bunker!

[This missive translated from [Untranslatable] to English. *When only the best* [Untranslatable] *will do, choose* [Untranslatable] *for all your galactic translations!*]

NOTICE OF IMPENDING FUMIGATION

People of Earth:

Your planet has been designated for fumigation. Please see below for details.

<u>Why is this happening?</u>
The Galactic Corporation at [Untranslatable] has determined that Earth is currently in the midst of an outbreak of [Untranslatable] *Flu*. (You may also know it as the [Untranslatable] *Fever*, [Untranslatable] *Plague*, or *The Crazypants*.) As you are aware, this disease is caused by a highly infectious, sentient pathogen, commonly known as [Untranslatable] or George.

As there is no known cure for [Untranslatable], the best recourse once an outbreak has occurred is to eradicate the infected populace.

<u>Is there a cure?</u>
There is no cure.

<u>Eradication seems drastic?</u>
Eradication is the only viable options to halt the spread. Those infected with [Untranslatable] seek only to find others to infect. Once a planet has run out of host candidates, the afflicted will exhaust all options to *leave* the planet for other worlds.

Any of those infected who are still capable will acquire spacecrafts, while the later-stage infected will instinctively gravitate to higher ground for as long as higher ground exists. We at the Galactic Corporation's corporate headquarters at [Untranslatable] have a responsibility to our shareholder planetary systems to step in *before* a runaway outbreak of [Untranslatable] Flu jumps planets.

<u>How will the planet be fumigated?</u>
Employing the latest and best technology, our expert team of fumigators will surround the planet with our patented *Neutron Shield* and irradiate the surface with high doses of gamma radiation.

This process uses 1/3 less gamma radiation than our competitors, with twice the effectiveness in half the time. (Ask for a brochure!) Your planet should be ready for repopulation in fewer than twenty-thousand galactic standard years, which is a lot better than the thirty-five thousand the competition can promise!

<u>When will this begin?</u>
The fumigation has not yet been scheduled. Expect a second notice closer to the date.

FOR SPECIAL CIRCUMSTANCES ONLY

<u>What do I do if my entire species is located on this planet?</u>
We at the Galactic Corporation at [Untranslatable] recognize that some less advanced species may be facing total extinction as a consequence of this outbreak. (Although this is rare.) If you have reason to believe our fumigation program will result in the cessation of your lifeform as a *whole*, please take the following steps.

1: Collect.
Gather all individuals you can prove, credibly, are uninfected.

2: Evacuate.
Leave the planet's surface immediately.

3: Assemble and remain self-isolated.
Find the nearest *uninhabited* orbital object—a moon, or a nearby asteroid—land and *wait*. You are now self-quarantining.

[IMPORTANT: Do *not* attempt to land on another inhabited planet. Now that the Galactic Corporation of [Untranslatable] has identified your world for fumigation, *all* craft originating from your home planet will be treated as hostile.]

4: Notify.
As soon as you've touched down, send word to your local Galactic Corporation corporate representative. Tell them what planet you are from and whether you require retrieval. Once the mandated quarantine period has elapsed, a representative will arrive to tend to your further needs.

Thank you for trusting the Galactic Corporation at [Untranslatable]!

***

To Whom It May Concern—

If you're reading this and I haven't shot you yet, it means I'm dead. Assuming the cabin I've attached this note to is still upright, you're welcome to what's inside.

I'm sure you're thinking this is real neighborly of me, and you're right, except that's how *I* got the cabin, and how the fellow before me got it too. Basically, somebody way back at the beginning of the contagion (probably *before* the contagion) stocked this place with everything needed to survive the end of the world and then the end of the world came and he didn't plan near as well as he thought he had, seeing as how he's dead now.

Anyhoo, it's a pretty sweet little place.

Probably. I mean, I may be dead inside, or alive but so happy I want to bite your face off. If I'm dead, bury me or whatever and I hope I didn't stink it up too much. If I try to bite you, I apologize for that but you know how it is with these Pantaloonies.

Here's some things I worked out about your new home.

First off, there's a bomb shelter under the cabin floor. I wouldn't've found it if the last guy hadn't tipped me off, so now I'm doing the same. You gotta roll up the rug. The handle's under the loose floorboard with the splintered end. Give it a good tug and there you go.

It's a decent shelter, not that I have any to compare it to. Damn shame the end of the world didn't involve bombs—not including when the government nuked New Mexico which, I mean, didn't even *work*. It's cement-lined, got its own generators, and that's where all the food is.

Second, there's no goddamn can opener.

I don't know what happened to it; maybe the first guy had one of them special pocket knives with an opener on it or something, but I have gone through this entire house top-to-bottom and it's just not here. The guy before me used a hunting knife to pop the cans, so I did that too. It's hard work, and I nearly lost a finger one time, but unless you've got an opener of your own it's probably the best you're gonna do.

Third, there's *plenty* of ammo, but not a single note about what goes where. Hopefully, you know from guns, but aside from the rifle I was planning to shoot you with I never worked out much. (I'll tell you one thing: smaller gun does NOT equal smaller bullets.) I'd have probably gotten further along, but I was afraid of using the guns too often. I didn't want to call attention to myself.

Fourth, there's some kind of coordinated gang of Pantaloonies roaming the countryside. Not sure why, because there's not a lot to see out here other than the observatory on the hill. (Which is locked, incidentally. I think there's people holed up in it, but I headed there before finding this cabin and I can tell you that if they're alive, they aren't open to visitors.) If you're going to spend a lot of time out of the shelter, I'd recommend figuring out the timing of that pack first; they're pretty regular.

Fifth, you're not gonna be able to spend *all* your time in the shelter, as much as that seems like a good idea. I think the designer messed up with the filtration system. Either that or something died in it. So unless you've got an HVAC degree and can fix it yourself, I'd moderate my time down there if I was you. (Then again, *I* didn't make it, so what do I know?)

Finally, and this isn't really related to the cabin, I've been seeing some pretty weird lights in the sky around here. Like, "alien spaceship" weird. They're probably here for the observatory too.

I wasn't brave enough to send a flare (the flare gun's in the shelter next to the peaches) on the chance they're on some kind of rescue mission or whatever, but maybe you'll be braver'n I was.

Oh, and the wood stove works, but you'll probably need wood for it, depending on when I died. There's an axe near the door.

Best of luck to you!

———————

[This missive translated from [Untranslatable] to English. *When only the best* [Untranslatable] *will do, choose* [Untranslatable] *for all your galactic translations!*]

APOLOGIES FOR OUR ERROR

People of Earth:

We at the Galactic Corporation at [Untranslatable] would like to apologize for our recent NOTICE OF IMPENDING FUMIGATION. Receipt of this message undoubtedly caused a panic.

It was sent in error.

Due to a clerical misclassification, your planet was categorized as Advanced. This was based on a survey of your unpopulated orbital satellites, frequent concentrated radiographic bursts directed away from the planet, and trace evidence of habitation on your nearby moon.

Now that we have received your numerous frantic (and profane) responses to our initial notification, it has come to our attention that you are *not* Advanced, and currently lack the technology to self-sustain off-planet for long periods.

The correct classification for your species is Intermediate. Had we known this, we would have sent no notification at all.
We apologize for the confusion.

Thank you for trusting the Galactic Corporation at [Untranslatable]!

[This missive translated from [Untranslatable] to English.
When only the best [Untranslatable] *will do, choose* [Untranslatable] *for all your galactic translations!*]

WE WILL OF COURSE HELP IN ANY WAY WE CAN!

People of Earth:

We apologize for the last two messages—NOTICE OF IMPENDING FUMIGATION and APOLOGIES FOR OUR ERROR.

Please allow us to explain.

Galactic Corporation's corporate policy dictates that we only notify species categorized as Advanced or higher of impending fumigation. Galactic Corporation's corporate policy *also* dictates that we make *no* contact with species categorized as *less than* Advanced under any circumstances. Finally, it is—as previously stated—Galactic Corporation's corporate policy that under no circumstances are we to directly interact with a planet with an [Untranslatable] Flu outbreak.

The previously-outlined accommodations in the event our fumigation was to cause the total extinction of a sentient species has been our *only* alternative assistance plan. However, we now recognize that proceeding with the fumigation as planned—and as policy dictates—creates significant reputational liability for the Galactic Corporation at [Untranslatable].

We have heard your complaints! And we are listening! (Indeed, it appears every remaining uninfected person on Earth has a radio transmitter and a colorful vocabulary. There is a lot to listen to!) Your spirited interest in remaining alive has captured the attention of our legal and public relations departments in particular, as well as the attention of the Office of Endangered Sentient Species on [Untranslatable] Six.

Very shortly, we will be dispatching five ships to Earth in advance of the fumigation, to the locations disclosed following this message. These locations were chosen because they appear to be empty of any humanoid lifeforms, which is the only way we can (hopefully) avoid anyone carrying the [Untranslatable] Flu.

All uninfected members of your species who can make it to one of the five locations at the specified time will be removed from the planet, quarantined remotely and then [Untranslatable] for long-term care.

We hope this solution is satisfactory, and that you are encouraged to stop using your radiographic devices.

Thank you for trusting the Galactic Corporation at [Untrans-latable]!

WE'RE SORRY WE MISSED YOU

From: The last of the human race
To: Everyone else

Hello!

We're sending this from aboard the last spaceship leaving Earth!

We'd like to say we hope this finds you well, but it probably doesn't.

We're sorry about this, but we tried to convince the aliens to make another trip, and we don't think we got through. Their translation program isn't all that hot and they're not a hundred percent sure which species they're even supposed to be talking to. I mean, they let us bring our dogs (dogs made it!) but then they spent our first three hours of the trip trying to talk to *them* instead of us. This was a real problem when it turned out they didn't know we needed to breathe oxygen.

If we're being honest, this whole rescue thing has been a fiasco from end to end. The aliens—they call themselves something that sounds like gargling, so we've been calling them the Gargles —seem pretty advanced, but not super-well-organized.

Just look at where they landed their ships. All of us here got on at the one that landed in Northern Canada, and we're pretty sure at least two or three people made it to the Sahara location, but that's about it. I mean, obviously, right? One landed on top of Mount Everest, another at the bottom of the Atlantic (they *really* didn't know what kind of species they were picking up,) and the fifth one in New Mexico, which is still super-radioactive.

They honestly looked surprised anyone showed up at all at the Canadian location. That is, if we're interpreting their facial expressions accurately. (Provided we're even looking at their faces; there are three anatomical possibilities.) The more cynical among us think the Gargles weren't really trying to rescue anyone at all, and they just guessed wrong about Canada.

Anyhow, we're here now and like I said, we're being told they can't go back to rescue anyone else, and we're really sorry about that. I guess the fumigation is impossible to reschedule, and they are *really* worried about this viral whatever, which is fair. Assuming you're listening to this live, they should be arriving to sterilize the whole planet in twenty-four hours.

So I guess this is it.

We wanted you to know that some of us made it. The human race will survive. Yes, all we have are Canadians—and whoever the Gargles scooped up in northern Africa (assuming they retrieved humans and not a bunch of camels)—but we're here, and we're okay.

We don't know where they're taking us, but they seem all right. I mean, we're not exactly in a position to do much if they decide we look delicious or whatever, but so far so good!
And hey, it sounds like the planet will be habitable again in

about twenty-thousand years, so that's something to look forward to, right? Something for our descendants to inherit, if they want it. Also, the fumigation won't destroy *things*, so if you want to write back, go ahead. Nobody will be able to read it for a *really* long time, but, I mean, it's something to do!

Anyway, we're all really sorry about how this worked out for the rest of you.

All the best!

Sincerely,
The last of the human race

ABOUT THE AUTHOR

Gene Doucette is the author of over twenty-five sci-fi/fantasy titles, including the Sorrow Falls series (*The Spaceship Next Door*, *The Frequency of Aliens*, and *Graffiti on the Wall of the Universe*), the Immortal series, *Fixer* and *Fixer Redux*, the *Tandemstar* books, and *The Apocalypse Seven*. Gene lives in Cambridge, MA.

For the latest on Gene Doucette, follow him online
genedoucette.me
genedoucette@me.com

www.ingramcontent.com/pod-product-compliance
Lightning Source LLC
Chambersburg PA
CBHW070459200726
48293CB00007B/2287